AN INHERITED PAST

The Forgotten Darkness Series

Demas Huckaba

ISBN: 978-1-4834-5345-3 (sc)
ISBN: 978-1-4834-5316-3 (hc)
ISBN: 978-1-4834-5315-6 (e)

Library of Congress Control Number: 2016909584

Lulu Publishing Services rev. date: 06/14/2016

ACKNOWLEDGEMENTS

Thanks to all the family and friends who inspired me along the way. I couldn't have done it without any of you. Also, a special thanks to my wonderful girlfriend who pushes me every day to be the very best I can be.

To Todd, my editor, you are one exceptional beaver.

A big thank-you to my parents for always being there for me and believing in me through all my challenges. I will love you both forever.

To one of my best friends, Jeffrey. Thank you for believing in me and helping me jumpstart this amazing journey. It's meant so much to me.

Prologue

The Start of War

Papers were strewn about the desktop in his office, each with equations more complicated than the last. Some were blueprints of what seemed to be highly advanced technological designs, while others seemed like a chaotic mess that only the incredibly brilliant could make sense of. However, he wasn't brilliant enough to figure out the perplexing problem right in front of his face.

"Allen?" A feminine voice came from across the office, causing him to jump slightly.

"Yes?" he replied as he regained his composure, his voice a little groggy from how tired he was. He had been spending every waking hour trying to work out every problem of this project, a project that was not even supposed to be messed with but one he led without wavering.

"It's ready. We can flip the switch anytime." These words put a smile on both of their faces. The time had finally come to put an end to the years of hard work. He looked down at the problem before him and pushed it aside. It would have to wait because it was time to make history. He made his way across the room and out the door that was held open by his colleague and into a large dome-like area filled with chatter.

Stalactites of natural rock mixed with advanced, intricate technology hung from the top of the dome. Across the cold floor of an unknown and alien metal, spread dark, imperfect grid-like patterns. They were broken and seemed to be placed sporadically. Desks and computers were set in appropriate places to study the surroundings, but the main, priceless jewel of his life was placed in the back. He stopped to stare. There was a short flight of stairs that led to a platform, and on either side of that was three diagonally angled spires that pointed to an empty point above the platform. The spires were far beyond the technology of humanity, which was apparent just by looking at them.

Voices died down as he reached a computer near the center of the room. All eyes were watching, and all ears listening for what was about to happen. The anticipation was palpable. He looked to the person he had been walking with as if to get an approval to continue. Upon receiving a nod, he cleared his throat loudly and called the attention of everyone in the area.

"Everyone!" he called out, a smile on his face. "Today is the day. After all of our years of hard work and secrecy, we can finally cross the finish line. Today we flip the switch and activate the artifact." He gave a long pause while looking over the gathered crowd, seeing smiles and looks of satisfaction spreading across their faces. Looking down at the computer in front of him, he pulled up a program and hovered his finger over the Enter key.

"Are you ready?" he yelled to the masses. Not even a moment later he was given yelps of joy, and the sound of clapping hands flooded the air. Once the noise and excitement hit its peak, he hit the button. His heart pounded as he waited for what was to come. Then it happened.

The lines on the floor lit up a bright green and began pulsing toward the product of all their hard work. The spires lit up with life every time a pulse reached them. Broken grid lines started to appear on the machinery hanging from the ceiling. Then something caught his attention. Blue light started to appear on the tips of the spires, but the light seemed different. It moved through the air and flowed like smoke that rippled with each pulse. Soon, it formed a bright white ball above the center of the platform with a pinpoint black core. Then, all the lights dimmed, and the sphere collapsed in on itself, leaving a tiny blackness the size of a baseball. There was silence as everyone looked on.

"Come on," he said quietly to himself as the seconds passed with no change. His heart started to pound, and a worried feeling crept in. Then it happened; brilliant blue cracks appeared all over the black ball, and rays of light burst forth. More and more appeared until it shattered. A white shockwave released upon the shell, breaking it, and washed over everything. It was so bright that it temporarily blinded everyone. Once the crowd's vision was regained, it could be seen: a large energy sphere the height of a two-story house. Its center was pitch-black and faded to a bright blue on the outer edges. Those edges wisped out like a mist and faded into nothing. The green lines that had been pulsing became calm.

His mouth was agape from the astounding power and beauty he had witnessed. Then the perplexing problem found its way back into his mind. He still had to test to see how bad it actually was.

"Great job, everyone," he shouted. "It works. Now shut it down, and we'll study our data. We'll start it up again tomorrow." People went about their usual business but were quickly stopped by a reply.

"Sir," someone spoke from a nearby monitor. "It won't shut down."

Dang it, he thought. "Have you tried everything?"

"Besides turning off all power, yes."

"Then try that."

The person got up from his seat and walked over to a box on the wall that had many switches. One by one, he flipped all of them, and as each of them were flipped, everything started going dark. Soon, every computer and piece of equipment was lifeless. All except for the artifact remained without power.

"All power is out!" Yet the mass of energy still floated, unwavering above the platform.

"It's self-sustaining," Allen whispered to himself as he looked on from where he had activated it only moments before. Before him was the problem that had perplexed him for many sleepless nights. A problem he hadn't been 100 percent sure would occur was confirmed before him. He had been too impatient.

"What do we do?" a scientist came up and asked.

"We leave it on and see where it goes from there, and watch it around the—" He was cut short as the sphere hummed deeply and seemed to vibrate him to his core. Suddenly, he looked to the bottom of the giant orb and saw that something had started to materialize out from it. First a head peeked through and looked around the room. The thing was far from human. It stepped all the way through and could be seen fully. The body resembled something of a starving dog mixed with a type of reptile. His eyes darted to three front claws with an extra-long center one that retracted back behind its forearm. Broken chains hung from its neck and wrists.

"It's a portal," Allen said as he stared at the horrific-looking creature. His heart started to beat hard. "Not a reactor."

There was silence as everyone looked on. The creature didn't move as it glared down at its potential prey. Then, without warning, it opened its long mouth with razor-sharp teeth and let out a blood-chilling scream. Immediately after, it jumped back into the portal, which gave another deep hum. Shock and awe filled the following moments as heartbeats rose.

"Find a way to turn it off now!" Allen yelled. Many were leaving the complex, but many stayed, determined to see their hard work through. They had given up everything possible for this.

"Sir, we didn't think it would self-sustain. We currently have no idea how to turn it off."

"No," he said to himself. He didn't want that creature coming back.

Another scientist walked up to him in a hurry with fear in her eyes. "I just called the military and informed them of everything. They're on their way."

"What did you do?" he bellowed in response. "We've been working in secrecy for a reason!"

"We're in over our heads," she began to cry. "I'm so sorry." She then turned around and walked away. The man was furious, but before he could even begin another thought, the portal began to hum deeply again. This time something different stepped through. Something more familiar. It was a man with a strangely-designed robe that pulsed with the same grid patterns that were seen across the floor and machinery. Then something unexpected happened: he spoke.

"Oh, you poor people," he began. His voice was smooth and calm yet deep.

"It speaks English?" a man close by whispered. "How is that even possi—" He was cut off as the cloaked figure raised a hand to silence the room completely.

Then the cloaked man continued, "When you find a shut door with no idea what is behind it, it is best not to open it. Now your stupidity has led to our salvation. But not yet." He turned around with a smirk and walked into the portal once more. Moments later, it began to hum more deeply than ever as countless creatures began to emerge, each locking eyes on a victim.

"There are so many of them," Allen said as his eyes widened in fear. His voice was barely audible. "Run," he choked. The instructions were unnecessary, however. A creature ripped a treacherous scream from its throat and shot forward toward the nearest person at an astonishing speed. Before impact, it stretched out its long middle claws and collided with the human's chest. Life left the human's eyes as he collapsed to the ground with blood soaking through his clothes. The creature looked up for its next target, and the others followed suit, each lurching for their own target.

Fearful screams and panic exploded from all in the dome as each was hunted down mercilessly. It was not long till the only sound was that of crunching bone and the sound Allen's own shaking breath. He had taken cover under a desk and hid from sight.

Everything raced through his mind. His family and his actions that had just gotten so many killed were a few among those thoughts. However, the main lingering thought was how long he had left. He had no idea how much time had passed since the onslaught. Time didn't even seem to exist. He knew only one thing: he had to get out. He listened closely and didn't hear any of the creatures nearby, but he knew that didn't mean they weren't watching.

Slowly, he peeked out from under his desk and instantly was met with the lifeless eyes of his colleague, who was lying still on top, a picture of her family crumpled in one hand, stained with her blood. Tears welled up in his eyes as he forced himself to look away and choke back a cry. Upon looking away, he saw his exit. He knew if he could get through the door and shut it that it might give him enough time to get out to safety.

He quickly ducked back under his desk as he heard one of the creatures come by. It jumped on top of the desk and rumbled a growl deep in its throat. The thought of "now or never" came to mind, and he went for it. He bolted toward the exit as fast as he could go. As soon as he was clear of the desk, he heard the creature release its shrill scream, which caused the others to release theirs. His heart was kicking in his chest as he ran. One of the things shot past him and shattered through a desk.

The door to his freedom wasn't far away, when his vision turned upward. One of the creatures had launched and wiped out his legs from under him. His back slammed against the ground at the same time the door burst open. Strong, shouting voices came running through, and loud bangs were accompanied by flashes of light. Before he knew it, his attacker was lying motionless beside him. The screams from the creatures rose to a chaotic roar and slowly died with each bang and flash. Suddenly, a pair of combat boots stepped in front of his face.

"What have you done?" the man yelled as the room reached silence. All that could be heard was the boots of soldiers running around to secure the area.

"All clear, Major Avery," a soldier called out from near the portal where many others had their weapons trained on the mysterious sphere.

"Answer me!" Avery bellowed at the man on the ground.

"We didn't know it was a portal." Tears began to form once more. "We thought it was some kind of reactor. It can't be shut down. It's self-sustaining. I had no idea this would . . ." His words cut off, and he went silent. The weight of his actions was coming down upon him.

Avery's eyes widened as he turned to look at the sphere that rose into the air. At least he knew it couldn't be shut down. He would have to find a way to keep the demon-like creatures from getting through. It was then that an idea occurred to him.

"Get him to a medical team, and I need a team to get these bodies out of here. Another needs to stand guard on the portal while another goes in," the major said. A soldier turned to the major.

"Wait, what?" The soldier didn't seem amused by the major's order at all.

"We're going through. If we can't shut this thing down, then we need to establish some type of base on the other side. Create a defense there and here. For all we know, there could be assets on the other side. We're going to make it ours," the major said.

CHAPTER 1

Just Getting Started

About three years earlier, a group of rogue scientists opened an ancient portal that led to a new planet that came to be known as Prison World. It had been recently determined that the portal could not be closed until the passing of five years. The country's military guarded the opposite entrance of the portal. Everything seemed calm at the time. However, more troops would soon be needed to prevent the nightmare from escaping into our world.

This information was all over the news, and that was why Damien was at the Prison World Defense System launch site. He was prepared to join the fight and make a difference in the war.

"Are you serious?" Damien spoke to himself as the global news was played on the nearest television. "They activated an ancient artifact without knowing how to close it or whether it could even be closed—or even knowing what it was? Haven't they heard of the expression, look before you leap?"

He was frustrated by the carelessness of the rogue team of scientists. Allowing those bizarre creatures, called Prisoners, to enter their world had led to the death of many people. He and his team were determined to make a big difference in the struggle with those monstrous creatures.

It had taken an entire year of constant training with his team, waiting for this opportunity, and he finally had been given a shot.

"Group number eighty-seven is next," called a woman seated at a desk across the room. She was typing behind a computer monitor.

That was Damien's group, which consisted of three people: himself, JD, and Peter. JD and Peter were close comrades of his, and even though their behavior sometimes didn't indicate it, together they formed one of the best teams in the special forces. JD was talented with long-range weapons, Peter was a close-quarters expert, and Damien was exceptional at close combat, specializing in medium to long ranges.

After acknowledging the call, Damien adjusted his dark-brown hair and beckoned to both JD and Peter. The team slowly arose from their chairs and approached the woman seated at the desk. Damien noticed JD grinning at Peter and knew what JD was about to do.

"Hello, beautiful," JD said with an attempted smoothness in his voice as he approached the woman and leaned against the desk.

The woman continued looking at the computer monitor, unfazed by the comment. "What are you going in as?" she asked, continuing to ignore JD's remark.

"Special forces or your boyfriend, whichever you prefer," he immediately answered, preempting replies from Damien and Peter. He flashed his hazel eyes at her in hopes that it may better his chances at her number.

"And your name is?"

"Jerimiah Koffee," he said as he grinned. "Smooth and bold."

Even though the woman ignored his remarks, she didn't seem bothered by them. She carried on looking at the monitor nonchalantly, and JD finally informed her that the team was SF5-3. She searched the computer's database for the group. After confirming the group, she directed them to a hallway and told them to enter through the last door on the right. As the group started toward the hallway, the woman, who had disregarded JD's facetious remarks seconds before, handed him a folded slip of paper.

"Follow this hallway all the way down until you reach a door on the right." The woman smiled and pointed. "When you reach it, you can go ahead and read the note."

"Should I be prepared to run back for a number?" JD asked, his voice full of hopefulness, but the woman just gave a small laugh and called for the next group.

The men went down the long hallway, which appeared to slant downward into the earth. Damien felt quite nervous. He figured that both JD and Peter were nervous as well. Even though JD would occasionally do a few small jumps in anticipation of the note, he knew JD was full of all kinds of emotions. The same went for Peter, who was humming some random theme song. The time had finally come for them to combat the Prisoners. They had diligently studied the creatures and gone through strenuous training to prepare for them.

After reaching the halfway point of the long hallway, Peter nudged JD's arm. "You should read her note now, buddy," Peter said with a grin.

"Oh, right, not like she'd know when I reach the door," JD replied, forming a smirk. He took the folded slip of paper from his pocket and read it. Immediately, he smiled and shook his head.

"So do you have a girlfriend to return to?" Damien asked jokingly.

"Probably not would be my best guess. Only in my dreams, based on the note." He laughed. He was used to situations like this.

"The score is now JD six and women 191!" Peter exclaimed.

"Are you joking, or have you seriously been keeping count?" Damien asked in response to Peter's comment.

"I kept track ever since the first time I witnessed a rejection of his," he said with a confident smile. "This wasn't long after we met each other. It's actually quite easy to keep count."

"Did you just have a feeling it was going to happen a lot so you made sure to keep track starting with rejection number one?" Damien laughed.

"Yeah, man."

"Well, I have no objections."

"I've been on a date more than just six times!" JD protested.

"No, you haven't," Peter replied.

"Yes, I have!"

"Nope."

The men finally reached their destination but paused before entering. There was no going back once they passed through the door's threshold. They didn't even contemplate the fact that going into the dangerous world would forever change their lives. Their minds had been made over a year before.

After a moment, JD slowly reached to open the door. Peter, with his stocky frame, was filled with enthusiasm and anxiously waited for the door to open. JD turned the handle and pushed the door forward. As the first steps were taken to enter what lay beyond, Peter pushed both Damien and JD with great force through the open door. The floor within the area had been cleaned shortly before, thereby making it slippery, and they quickly fell onto each other.

"Thanks, Peter." Damien sighed under the weight of their teammate.

"No problem."

The men got back on their feet and looked around. They were inside a dome of great expanse, an area that could not be seen from outside the building. It was underground, Damien realized. At a distance, near the back, was the portal, which the team noticed was immense. It was spherical, with energy jolting from its edges. The center of the portal exhibited a darkness beyond what one is used to seeing, an extreme, ominous blackness. This was the ride to that world, a world in which they would soon reside while engaged in war. It was truly astonishing.

The surrounding technology within the dome was also impressive. It was technology that neither seemed to have been manufactured by contemporary human minds nor could be. The dome had a large group of scientists seated at advanced computers and others attending to matters incomprehensible to Damien and the others. Platoons were lined up in front of the massive portal in sets. As each platoon proceeded forward into the portal, it appeared as if the soldiers vaporized into nothingness. The portal emitted a deep hum each time a platoon entered it.

Many human-made turrets were pointed toward the portal. Damien knew this had to be a safety protocol in case the portal were breached from the other side by the enemy. Besides the turrets and the troops entering the portal, there were several soldiers walking around the dome with weapons drawn, ready for combat at a moment's notice.

The men on the team were amazed, but Damien was especially impressed by the unfolding scene. Watching troops completely vanish filled him with awe. It would soon be their turn to enter it, he thought. During training, instructors assured him that entering the portal was completely safe. However, as he watched men enter the portal, his confidence of that assurance slightly weakened.

A scientist who was short and thin approached Damien's group with a clipboard in hand. "To what group do you belong, sir?" asked the scientist.

"Group SF5-3," Damien immediately replied, snapping out of his overwhelmed state.

He tried to give himself an air of professionalism and confidence, which didn't seem to be of any consequence to the scientist before him.

The man took a pen from his lab coat and wrote on his clipboard. "You're behind schedule," the scientist remarked with slight annoyance while shaking his head. "Please proceed to the transportation line."

"Behind schedule? We waited in the upper lobby and came here once we were called. We're on time," Damien insisted.

The scientist walked away without acknowledging his reply, and the team followed the order regardless.

The man's behavior had slightly annoyed Peter, and he decided to substitute that annoyance with amusement. He dug into his pockets for anything he could use. It took just a moment before he pulled out a rubber band and devised a plan to use it on the scientist. As he quietly approached the man from behind, Damien noticed what he was up to. He quickly notified JD of Peter's antics, and both silently observed. As Peter snuck up behind the scientist, the scientist paused for a moment to write on his clipboard, and Peter pounced at the opportunity. He fully stretched the rubber band, his brown eyes narrowed on his target, and fired it at the scientist's neck at point-blank range. The rubber band produced a conspicuous sound that caused other scientists in the vicinity to turn to see from where it came. Peter's rubber band struck the scientist's neck with such force that a welt had already begun to appear. The unsuspecting victim reached for the back of his neck as a reflex and spun around. He saw Peter grinning and realized he was the only one who could have done it. As soon as he came to that realization, the team, laughing, was already dashing toward the portal with Peter close behind. Angered, the scientist gave chase.

As they rushed to the portal, Damien noticed the floor beneath his feet. It had green lines running everywhere. The lines were either horizontal or vertical, and each had a different pattern as it pulsed outward from anywhere his feet collided with the floor. It was like a pulsing green grid with multiple designs. The portal hummed and vibrated the air, making one's skin tingle. Diagonal pillars, each of intricate machinery, pointed to the portal. The tips on each pillar shone blue, and rippled air seemed to travel from them to the portal. As the team drew closer to the portal, the humming grew deeper and deeper, vibrating their core.

JD turned around to see whether the scientist was still chasing them or not. To his surprise, the scientist was close behind. Who would have thought the thin man would be able to run almost as fast as them, he thought, but soon the scientist started to fall behind. He was not made to keep up.

"I'm first!" JD exclaimed, pushing Peter to reach the portal before him, causing him to trip and fall.

He ran up the steps, past the other troops, and into the portal without a moment's hesitation. After he entered, his body vaporized, and the portal gave another deep hum and increased in brightness momentarily.

"Oh yeah!" shouted Peter as he got up from his fall.

The scientist noticed Peter and ran toward him, still angry. He managed to barely touch the back of Peter's shirt. However, Peter dashed away from him and entered the portal before the scientist could retaliate any further. The man, exhausted, stopped to catch his breath. Damien was the only one left to enter the portal, and he took the opportunity to admire it. The scientist didn't seem to concern himself with Damien. He wanted Peter, the person who made him angry, and seeing that his chance for revenge had gone, he stormed off to complete his duties.

The portal was massive, at least ten meters tall, and machines surrounded both its back and sides. While the portal in which he would enter was black, the outside was a brilliant blue that matched his eyes. As he stood within one step of the portal, he felt the energy resonating from it. The energy gave him a wonderful feeling and seemed to reduce the slight fatigue the running engendered. Immediately, a hand extended from the blackness and grabbed him by the shirt. Before Damien could react, the hand yanked him into the portal.

As he went in, he felt his body dematerialize, and the sensation was indescribable. His mind went blank immediately after. When he came to, he was face to face with Peter, on the other side of the portal.

"Seriously, dude!" Damien said. His eyes were wide, and he bent over. He didn't how to react to being taken apart at a molecular level and reassembled somewhere else.

He turned back to face the portal from where he had just come. Slowly, he stuck his hand in and observed. It took itself apart and seemed to turn into a mist the further he stuck it in. He could still feel and move. However, it became increasingly number near the end of his arm. Suddenly, he felt someone give him a high five on the other end. He pulled his hand back through, when he was interrupted and spun around by Peter.

Damien wanted to examine the portal more, but at that point all he had to admire was his teammate's face. There wasn't too much to admire either. He noticed the new location was a room that also had a few scientists around and soldiers with weapons stationed at every doorway. Before he could say anything more to Peter, a high-ranking officer approached them. The man seemed very familiar, but he couldn't place his face at the moment.

"Specify your group," commanded the officer.

Damien sighed. He had been asked to identify his group multiple times and was beginning to wonder how many more times he was going to have to do so.

"SF5-3," he replied in an annoyed tone.

"Hmm." The officer hesitated a moment while looking at Damien before continuing, "You're late."

The officer was an older man, perhaps in his mid-fifties. He had short, gray hair and walked with a slight limp. His uniform was clean and decorated with various medals.

"What! We are not late! We are right on time," Damien said loudly.

At once the officer gave a single, swift kick to Damien's groin. Instantly, his legs gave out and tears welled up in his eyes. Shortly after, his stomach twisted itself into knots and his eyes sealed shut. He realized too late that his remarks were out of line for speaking to a superior officer.

"Don't forget your place, soldier," said the officer. "Welcome to hell. Follow me."

The officer had a nefarious smile on his face as he turned to lead the way. Damien was still keeled over on the ground as JD and Peter stared with wide eyes. Some of the scientists not far from them chuckled, prompting them to laugh as well. The laughter soon ended, and both JD and Peter helped Damien up. With regained composure, Damien, along with his teammates, followed dutifully behind the officer, leaving the portal room.

The officer was already outside the room by the time they caught up. He was checking an old-fashion pocket watch while waiting for the men. When the team came out, he directed them to follow. They made sure to keep a good distance from the officer. JD and Peter, especially, kept their distance. They didn't want to suffer the same fate as Damien had. He was still surprised by the action. Being yelled at by a superior officer is to be expected for such actions but never receiving a kick in the groin. He was going to have to be a lot more careful from that moment on. The installation seemed to have its own set of rules, different from those one may be accustomed to on Earth.

As he contemplated this, he glanced at the sky. He immediately noticed that it wasn't bright blue like the skies of Earth. It was instead a grungy orange with tinges of blue mixed in, resembling a beautifully painted masterpiece. There was no sun, but everything seemed bright, as if one were present. It caused him to wonder if a moon or even stars would be present. There were clouds, however, that towered into the sky and reflected the light of the world. The characteristics of the world confused Damien, but he knew that it was a different world that he wasn't expected to fully understand. He decided to focus on what was at hand, but the thought of how much the planet resembled Earth stayed in the back of his mind.

The group eventually came to what seemed like an apartment complex of some sort. It was just one of many, however, and the military installation was full of them. Each one was needed to house all of the soldiers who were stationed there for the war. The complex seemed like it was constructed of some advanced alien technology resembling that of the dome that housed the portal. Damien didn't believe that the human race had become technologically advanced enough to produce it. Everything was well designed and visually pleasing. However, the architecture seemed perfectly designed for humans. The thought then occurred to him that the military may have produced new technologies for the war.

"I hope it's nice and has TV," JD said, breaking Damien's chain of thought.

"It's horrible," the officer stated. "It has no entertainment besides what you have in your standard issue bags."

The officer mentioned this right after JD's remark, giving the impression that he was eavesdropping. First impressions are important, and the officer hadn't given the team much to like about him thus far. However, they weren't giving him much to like either.

"We do not have any bags, sir," JD replied, still keeping his distance, with his hands folded over his lower area.

The officer turned around and examined the team.

"Why not?" he asked while raising an eyebrow. "You should have been issued bags before coming here."

"Well, we were kind of in a rush, being late and all."

"A moment ago you said you were right on time," the officer snapped. "Why were you in a rush?"

"Didn't you say we were late, sir?"

"That's not the point."

"Uh, we couldn't wait to come to this world and kill Prisoners?" JD said unconvincingly while glancing toward Peter as though he was asking for some assistance.

"Your grave." Peter grinned in response.

"It doesn't matter," the officer said, giving off a sigh. "We will supply you with your bags ASAP. Here is your room's key card for now."

The group reached the large entrance of the apartment complex, which had a rounded archway. Soldiers came in and out, going about their day-to-day duties, some leaving on missions while others seemed to be returning from battle.

"Here is a map of the military installation," the officer said. "Be sure to be up at 0500 and at the armory at 0600. Tomorrow is going to be a long day for you, girls. Get some rest." He turned around to leave but then immediately stopped and looked over his shoulder. "And, Damien, you need to watch yourself a little more. I've heard better of you." When he finished speaking, he continued on his way but left Damien really confused. He didn't know why the officer had been so formal with him and still couldn't understand why he had seemed so familiar. A thought was

9

forming in the back of his mind that he knew the officer from somewhere, but he knew he hadn't seen him anywhere on official military business.

The officer left the team with an air of contentment. He probably enjoyed messing with them. However, they didn't let it bother them much. Boot camp had been far worse. The whole ordeal seemed to be moving along very quickly. So quickly, in fact, that it didn't seem proper. But the team was fine with it. They didn't care for being uptight and proper, and it had worked for them so far.

No mission briefings were given. They figured everything would be explained the following day or at whatever time was convenient for the ones in charge. Damien was ready to get started and took a step forward. As the team entered the complex, their jaws dropped in unison. They couldn't believe their eyes. It was like a five-star hotel inside. It had game rooms, snack counters, and bars. Large sophisticated TVs occupied the walls for viewing pleasure.

"Well," JD began with a sigh, "he's a liar, but I'm not mad. Maybe he lied about getting up early tomorrow, too."

"Let's not take the chance," Damien replied.

As they gazed at the scenery, Damien noticed a clock that indicated that it was 7:00 p.m. The day had gone by very quickly, but he wasn't yet tired, so he decided to go check out the room. He informed his teammates of this.

"You two can do what you want, but remember to get up at 0500," he said.

"Yeah," Peter said.

"Gotcha," JD replied as they kept looking around, jaws agape.

"I don't want a repeat of the incident we had at that one hotel last month. Deal?"

"No promises," Peter said in a hushed voice.

"Peter . . ."

"Fine. No flooding the lobby for slip n' slide purposes."

"Wait, what?"

"Oops, wrong time. You meant the other time that we—"

"When did you do that?" Damien asked with his voice raising a bit in pitch. He had never heard of that. Peter started laughing, and JD joined in.

"He's just joking," JD chuckled. "We never did that. Just giving you a hard time. We'll behave."

"You better be," Damien said in relief. "Have fun."

"Will do."

The men went their separate ways exploring the establishment. Damien walked across the lobby and eventually spotted an elevator. The room key had 397 engraved in a shining silver on it, and according to the map beside the elevator, room 397 was on the third floor. He entered the elevator and selected the appropriate floor. As the elevator doors were closing, a girl slipped in. Damien stepped to one side to make room for her and couldn't help but notice how beautiful she was. She was a young woman with brown hair and bright blue eyes. She was just slightly shorter than he was, and her hair reached her shoulders. She wore jeans, and a T-shirt with a design that was very artistic. He had expected to ride the elevator alone, but he didn't mind sharing it with such an attractive woman. Suddenly, his gut tightened and his cheeks filled with a slight red tint. He knew her.

The young woman reached over and pressed for the second floor. Damien became slightly nervous. He initially chalked his nervousness up to the fact that he didn't know anyone there except JD and Peter. However, by that time, there were two people that seemed familiar, and he definitely knew her. As the two rode the elevator, Damien noticed that she quickly glanced at him. He wondered what she was thinking. He wondered if maybe she had remembered him as well. A moment later the elevator doors opened, and as she walked to leave, she looked at him.

"Bye," she said with a smile as she pulled a piece of her hair back behind her ear.

Damien was speechless and didn't know what to say. He gave her a quick smile and replied back with a bye of his own. She left the elevator and the doors closed, but before they did, he noticed her look back with a look of realization. Once the doors were shut, he heard her speak loudly through the door.

"Find and meet me at the vending machines in a little bit, Damien!"

"Alright," he yelled back in response as a smile spread across his face. He gave a sigh of relief, felt the hard beating of his heart, and leaned against the elevator doors for a moment before they opened once more, for his floor. He stepped into a hallway and looked at the doors that lined the halls, each with their own room number. He turned right and proceeded to room 397. Along the way, he thought of the girl. He was surprised to see her and even more surprised she was in the military. He wondered what all had happened to her since they had quit talking. As he came to his room door, he noticed a scanner. He pulled out his room key card and swiped it.

"Welcome, team SF5-3. Please enter," a computerized voice said from the scanner, followed by the sound of a few different beeps and a click.

He opened the door and proceeded into the room. The room was more than he expected it to be. It was quite large and had three large beds, each with their own mini fridge and TV. There was a balcony, and Damien promptly went to it. The balcony allowed one to see out into the city and the landscape beyond it. Even then, war was taking place. Gun towers were being constructed, and occasional flashes of gunfire could be seen at a far distance, lighting up pieces of the surrounding forest. Wind blew against him. He looked downward and gazed at the military city. Then he looked at the sky, which, surprisingly for him, displayed stars and a moon. A pleasant surprise, he thought. Damien recalled being informed that Prison World was all that was within this dimension. Confused, he searched the sky for any familiar constellations. To his astonishment, he was able to identify several. He couldn't understand how that was possible. It confused him even more that the night sky held the moon and stars, while the daytime held no sun. He pondered the situation for a moment but decided to not let it bother him. He was finally there, in the world he heard so much about while training, and the excitement he felt motivated him to explore more of the complex.

He left the balcony and his room in search of the vending machines. After going into the hallway, he turned left. As he wandered, he came to a room with stairs that led to what seemed to be a fitness area. There were various exercise machines available, many of which were foreign to him. He noticed a row of vending machines a few meters away. As he walked toward them, the girl he saw earlier in the elevator appeared.

"Hello again," she said with a smile.

"Hey, Moriah," Damien replied while receiving a hug from her. It had been so long since he had felt her embrace.

"How have you been?" she asked while stepping back into place.

"I've been pretty good. Obviously joined the military." He laughed a little.

"I noticed. My father also told me that you'd be coming here soon. I just couldn't recognize you. You've changed quite a bit."

"Your father?" he questioned instantly. The answer unlocked in his mind right before she answered him, and his eyes widened.

"Yes, he's Major Avery. You only met him a couple times when we were younger."

"Oh yeah. I met him today. He was"—he paused to recollect—"pleasant." The word didn't roll off his tongue so easily. At least he finally knew why the major had known his name, but he didn't want to talk about the events that occurred earlier.

"So how have you been?" he asked. "I haven't seen you since we were in high school."

"I know, right? We were supposed to be friends forever. Now we barely recognized each other. Anyway, I've been good, but I'll have to talk more later. Actually have to get up early to report to headquarters. Pretty busy here."

"I gotcha," he replied. "It was really great to see you again. Any chance of getting together sometime and catching up?"

"Of course!" Moriah exclaimed while she gave him one last hug. "We'll definitely run into each other again, so I'll tell you a good time to then." Her grip tightened and her tone lowered. "Just stay safe."

She pulled away and looked him in the eyes with a smile. It was in that moment that reality hit him. He couldn't promise his safety. He would be fighting a battle many had died in, and all Moriah wanted was for him to be safe. A request that when they were younger would seem so small but at that moment seemed almost impossible. However, he knew he had to say it.

"I'll be fine," he said, comforting her with a smile of his own. It seemed to warm her up inside, and her smile returned. "See you around?"

"I rarely leave the installation, so that shouldn't be a problem," she said as she turned to walk away. "Have a good night!"

"You, too, and stay safe as well!"

The two went their separate ways, and Damien thought about his interaction with her as he walked back to his room. He couldn't believe he had just run into her, on a military installation in another dimension.

Feelings that had lain dormant for years were slowly stirring deeply within him. She had been his crush as a teen and had grown ever more beautiful. He looked forward to the next time he would get to talk to her.

When he got back to the room, JD and Peter were still not there. They were probably still too excited to go to sleep, he thought. So long as they kept out of trouble, he was fine with it. He figured they would come to the room after he had fallen asleep. Damien closed his eyes, ready to finally get some rest. He gave a faint smile.

"We're just getting started," he whispered.

CHAPTER 2

Recon

Damien had slept very well during the night. He was in such a deep sleep that almost nothing could have disturbed him, even both JD and Peter coming in during the early hours complaining about him having the best bed, which could be manually adjusted in both its temperature and firmness. Unbeknownst to them, the bed was reserved for team leaders. Their complaints weren't enough to awaken him, however. After fussing, JD and Peter went to bed themselves.

A high-pitched whistle screeched throughout the entire apartment complex at five in the morning. The noise immediately stirred JD and Peter awake. Peter, with his usual smile and eyes wide open, sat on the side of his bed as if he had been waiting for the moment. JD was still lying in bed and had a pillow over his head in an attempt to alleviate the noise. Much to his surprise, it would not be much protection from Peter, who jumped on him in an attempt to get him out of bed. JD let out a groan after receiving a hard belly flop and immediately launched the pillow with full force, hitting the side of Peter's face and knocking him off the bed. The loud thud from Peter's fall made Damien stir. He uncovered himself and sat on the side of his bed, rubbing his eyes. With wide eyes, he looked over his shoulder at his team. They paused mid-action to stare back. JD had Peter in an arm lock with his face pressed against the bed. The whistle that had been going on for a couple of minutes had quit, and as if on cue, the two relaxed and returned to their own beds.

"Match over!" Peter exclaimed, with his hands in the air as he walked away. "Victory."

Damien rested his head in his hands. "How are we classified as professionals?"

"Don't ask me," JD replied as if he was part of the conversation. Damien stared at him through the gaps between his fingers.

The team's first objective was to go to the armory, which, according to the installation map, was approximately half a mile away from the apartment complex. There were four armories total on base, and the one they were headed for was located by a gate that led out of the city. With the whistle as their wake up call, the team finished getting ready. Damien was dressed in non-combative military gear. He believed that he would obtain combative gear at the armory. JD and Peter were dressed in standard military attire as well, which was different shades of gray and dark blue, with an elegant and modern style. Each had the special forces symbol stitched on each shoulder, and "SF5-3" was on the left side of their chest.

The team headed out of their room, down the elevator, and out into the lobby. Attendants were cleaning a mess that Damien suspected was probably due to his teammates. The glares the attendants gave both JD and Peter was a good sign. Damien looked around for Moriah, hoping he would see her before leaving for the armory. He didn't know what he would say to her, but he knew seeing her would be great. He figured he would probably be able to after visiting the armory. He didn't know how long the day was going to be, but he was more than ready.

To move toward the armory, the team headed south of their complex. As they were walking, JD and Peter became bored, as they usually did. That happened when there wasn't much for them to do. To appease their boredom, they would play a game of tag but in their own way. One would start the game by punching the other in the arm and running off. The other would give chase and try to catch up to hit back. If by chance one couldn't catch up and the other got away, then the one who couldn't catch up would have to find the other one. That is where things got interesting. Damien was always curious as to where they would hide or how they would even do it. He had seen Peter run around a corner without being seen and quickly scale the side of a building in whatever way he found possible and sit on the closest window ledge as JD ran under looking for him.

Damien didn't completely approve of the game because it could affect the team's timeliness in arriving at their destination since they would run off out of sight and could lose their way in a completely new area. However, knowing his teammates, not much could be done. He would have to trust them, hoping he wouldn't have to deal with repercussions due to their actions. Their excitement was understandable.

Along the way, Damien thought of Moriah and the past they had shared. He remembered her being against joining the military because it seemed that was her only choice because of her family. She had had other plans for life. He remembered a few nights that he and she had stayed up talking. They shared their dreams, and one of hers was dance. He wondered what had happened to that. He smiled as more and more memories slowly kept emerging from deep inside. Never did he realize how much he had missed all those times, until that moment.

Soon the armory was in sight and so were his teammates. They were walking around a corner near the armory and heading toward Damien. He shifted his gaze from them to his destination. It was quite high tech, with sleek designs and water pouring out of odd shaped blocks in the front of the building. A walkway with small pillars on each side led to the entrance, and each pillar had water that flowed from the top into a puddle beneath them. At the top of each pillar were floating rings of water of various sizes. The smaller ones spun in different directions inside the larger ones. The sight of them made him pause and wonder how it was done. The water was simply floating in air and would disperse and reform into the rings. He didn't expect it, but it was a nice sight.

Upon entering the armory, the team observed all sorts of weaponry. There was everything from a compact knife to a rocket launcher. The team then saw a man who appeared to be waiting for them.

"You're late," he announced in a deep voice.

The deep voice didn't go well with his appearance. The man was short, no more than five feet tall, and dressed in the same military attire as Damien but with different respective patches that defined who he was and his role. He had poor teeth and his hair was quite scraggly. Peter's face

17

turned red as he began laughing at the man's appearance. It seemed that the man knew why he was laughing, but he still looked quite surprised by Peter's actions.

"Sorry, sir," Damien apologized, with Peter still laughing behind him. "Lieutenant!" he yelled. "Control yourself."

JD decided to stop Peter before he could even follow orders, by putting him in a sleeper hold, which ended up being quite effective. He placed Peter on the floor and joined Damien.

"Was that necessary?" Damien asked.

"We'll brief him later," he proclaimed as he stood at attention with a grin. His gaze focused on the small man, and he turned slowly to Damien with an even bigger grin.

"No," Damien said with a straight face. The smirk disappeared just as quickly as it had appeared. He became very focused on the task at hand. When it came to mission briefings and other related matters, Damien could count on JD to respond appropriately.

"Let's keep this short," the man replied.

"That shouldn't be a problem," JD immediately answered with a returning grin while turning once more to Damien, whose face was unwavering. "Still no? Fine."

"I'm Frank," the man announced with a sigh. "I'm the one who runs this armory, and you have been ordered to come here, and I am to give you weapons. I have them ready for you. I have been ordered to give you a recon mission as well. Shall we begin?" He motioned to a table with packets of paper.

"Yes, sir," Damien answered as he made his way to the table. Frank waited until they were all situated at the table to begin.

"Dr. Quentin Wright, a research scientist, was sent on a mission. He was escorted by a couple of soldiers to his location and was attacked halfway to their destination. Only one of the soldiers came back alive. We have been informed by him that Dr. Wright was taken, but his current condition is unknown. It has been decided that your team would rescue him; however, if he is no longer alive, at least try to bring back his belongings. His research is classified, and all you need to know is that it is deemed very important. This mission will surely put your training to the test. Any questions?"

"What makes our three-man team different from his two-man escort team, and why wasn't a valuable asset better protected?" JD asked as he crossed his arms.

"We believed that their route was safe. All signs indicated that not many Prisoners were in the area. Even the few that were could have been taken out covertly without drawing the attention of many others. It seemed like a quick mission that didn't require a large team. With your team, you have one more capable person able to attack and defend."

"How do we know this isn't a suicide mission?" Damien butted in.

"Nothing is ever guaranteed on this planet, and you knew that signing up," Frank began in response. "Countless 'safe' lives have been claimed to keep us 'safe.' Fact is, even though we have been here for years, the behavior of the Prisoners is so sporadic we can't accurately predict it. There's a reason why more troops are needed all the time. The reason your team is being sent is because you are highly trained, and if we are to lose you, then we are only losing three instead of an entire squad of ten or more." The words didn't sit well with Damien, but all of them were true. He couldn't help but think of how Moriah would take it, or even his own family, if he were to die. However, he was the one who signed up for the job while knowing the risks. He couldn't complain.

"Questions?" Frank asked while surveying the faces of the two in front of him.

"Got a map?" Damien responded as he looked down at the intel in front of him.

"Coordinates are marked at the location where we believe he has been taken," Frank said as he handed Damien a map he had been hiding in his back pocket. "Any more questions regarding your mission?"

"None at all," Damien replied.

"Good. The mission begins as soon as you leave this building."

The words struck Damien with an uneasiness as he thought of Moriah. Already he was being sent on a possible death mission, and he couldn't even say goodbye. He knew he would have to keep his confidence that he would make it home and be able to see her again. He had so much he wanted to talk to her about.

Damien and JD quickly memorized all of their instructions, and both were getting ready for the next topic at hand, namely weaponry.

"Now for your weapons," Frank said. "I must warn you that each of these weapons is made out of very special materials that we have only been able to find in small quantities on this planet. Therefore, you break it and you don't get another one. I know each of you haven't seen actual battle, but you have received the highest score and praise from those who taught you. You even rose in ranks at a rapid rate due to that. I expect you to do well with these weapons. Anyway, each of you will carry a rapid-shot pistol, each with a twenty-round magazine and two spare. The bullets are hollowpoints, which will fire as fast as you pull the trigger."

"Sounds good," JD said, waiting for the good stuff.

"That's the standard weapon for all teams on this planet. It is the only weapon you'll be receiving that isn't made specially. The next weapon is designed for a mid-long range specialist. It's a sniper with a modified barrel that changes from long to mid range within 1.43 seconds at the flip of a switch. Also, all of your weapons have had Gauss technology implemented to allow near-silent firing. Recent advancements have been made to push that technology even further. You'll just have to see it for yourself."

JD smiled while listening to Frank's description. That would be his weapon.

"Next we have the multi-purpose rifle, which is for the team leader. This rifle can switch from semiautomatic to fully automatic with the flip of a single switch. The magazine holds seventy-five compact hollow rounds. The weapon effectively allows the user to decide when it will be a rifle or machine gun. The best part is that it is the latest in Gauss technology, like I said. Due to using electromagnetism as its source of propulsion for each round, you get almost absolute silence. The only thing you'll hear from your weapons is a small pop rather than a loud bang. There have been other advancements as well to make the internal operations quiet. Needless to say, the only sound those Prisoners will hear is their friends getting dropped."

Damien had a grin spread on his face as he wondered about the feel of firing the weapon. He took it in his hands and inspected it. A scope with an adjustable zoom rested on its top. He was highly impressed and found it to be the perfect weapon for him. The empty magazine was practically begging to be filled with ammo. Frank examined the expressions of both men as he explained each weapon, and he figured that both guns were well suited for them.

"Last but not least is the weapon for the close-quarter combat specialist," he went on. "It is a rapid fire, twelve-round shotgun that fires solid steel slug rounds. Recoil is almost nothing, as well, but there is something special about this weapon. Not only can it fire a solid, magnetic round, but it can also fire traditional shells for wider spread damage. The recoil for traditional rounds is more than the other, but we have done our best to reduce that recoil as well. I have a hard time believing that he is going to utilize this weapon," he said disapprovingly, glancing at an unconscious Peter on the floor.

The team received the rest of their equipment, which included SICKs, that is, standard issue combat knives, and various survival gear. Eventually Peter became conscious again, and his teammates briefed him on their mission as well as the equipment they received.

"Oh yeah, Christmas came early," Peter exclaimed as he staggered off the ground only to fall over again. Damien looked over his shoulder and saw Frank shake his head and turn away.

With their gear equipped, the team made its way to the main gate that loomed over the buildings that stood before it. Damien observed the bright orange sky with its tinges of blue, and felt a bit uneasy from the sight of dark clouds forming in the distance, but he decided to not worry himself over possible rainfall. Thinking optimistically, he considered how rainfall would provide cover and allow his team to accomplish its mission more effectively. Moriah also crossed his mind once more. He planned on speaking to her again after the mission. Since having seen her again, feelings continued to stir that made him feel light and warm.

The team was standing before the main gate, and both JD and Peter were conspicuously silent. Neither had spoke a word since leaving the armory nor did they resort to their usual hijinks. It must have been due to the fact that it was their first mission on a different planet, Damien thought. Something that new would get to anyone. His teammates were probably deep in thought just as he was.

The main gate was very tall, perhaps over one hundred fifty feet high, with electrified barbed wires running along its top. A wall, which was as tall as the gate, surrounded the entire installation, and turrets with motion sensors were strategically placed around it. It was meant to prevent Prisoners from infiltrating, Damien learned, especially Screamers, the most common type of Prisoner. They had been known to climb trees and leap the walls to infiltrate. That problem had ceased since the turrets were introduced.

He remembered the physical description of the Screamers. They had long legs, which gave them incredible running speed, and their mouths were lined with keen-edged teeth. Mysterious shackles were often seen attached to their neck, waist, wrists, or ankles. Their offensive ability wasn't to be underestimated. Fortunately, those trained to fight them would have no problem taking them down.

A scanner, in the form of green light, scanned the team as they approached the gate, and scanned the surrounding area outside of the gate as a precautionary measure.

"Authorized," was heard from it, and it henceforth opened. Damien and his teammates then had the opportunity to observe the landscape in person, and upon inspection, it seemed quite like their home world. The trees, however, were very tall. The density of them reminded one of a jungle, except for the dreadful screams that could be heard from deep within. The screams were from Screamers, no doubt, Damien concluded. The gate soon closed behind the men, and the disturbing screams ceased. That was a bit disconcerting to the team. Perhaps the Screamers decided to quiet down in order to pounce upon potential prey. The strange, new world the men entered was full of dangerous creatures, and their recon mission required that they dive deep into it.

"I'd like to see if I can bring back a Prisoner as a pet," Peter said randomly while they walked a trail that led away from the base. "That would be cool."

"Why? So it could kill you in the middle of the night?" JD said.

"It's so I can ride one like a horse, of course! Duh!"

"I cannot help but sometimes think that there's something wrong with you, Peter."

"I know."

That was another odd conversation between JD and Peter, Damien thought. He would usually join in on them, but he was somewhat nervous. As the team walked, his nervousness dissipated. He was part of a qualified team, and this was their first mission. There was neither time nor need to be nervous.

"Seriously, though," Peter continued, "they have been proven to be intelligent. We may classify most as animals, but even the Screamers have shown that they can devise and execute their own tactics. I believe that if done correctly, I can turn one into a pet."

"If these things were capable of reason and not just bloodthirsty killing machines, then don't you think we would have had a breakthrough on that front by now?" JD retorted.

"Maybe we just haven't taken the right approach."

"Well, be sure to tell me when you tame a killer." Peter had no response, but Damien knew that wasn't the end of things.

A canopy of thick, lush trees was getting closer at the end of the trail, and the men drew their pistols awaiting action. They were fully alert, and the slightest movement or sound would not escape their notice.

It wasn't long until JD signaled them to halt. Damien quickly scanned for the reason and spotted a Screamer glaring at them from a far tree. It was absolutely still and seemed to have been waiting for the team to come within attacking range.

"Time to test out my weapon," JD whispered as he brought his sniper up to aim. He soon had his target in sight and slowed his breathing as he rested his finger on the trigger. On his next exhale, he pulled. There was a pop, and the next thing that was heard was a thud in the distance. Damien focused back on the Screamer to find it was falling from its perch. A patch of blood left a piece of the trunk behind it stained.

"Nice shot," Damien responded in a low voice as he scanned the trees ahead of them for more hostiles.

As they moved forward, something caught Peter's eye. Another Screamer was moving through the trees above them. Its movements were nearly inaudible. He was able to determine that it was there despite its attempt to be covert, and he decided to attempt something. He got the attention of his teammates as the creature moved toward a low branch, and Damien and JD took notice of it. Peter clearly had a plan to take care of it and snapped his fingers twice and held his hand out flat toward them to convey that. The Screamer moved closer to Peter, and he reacted by stopping in front of a bulky tree, turning to face the creature. Once the

Screamer realized that his position was compromised, it immediately got into position and pounced at him, giving out a frightful scream. It aimed at Peter's chest with its massive claws, and he dodged it with a fraction of a second to spare. The creature's claws deeply pierced the trunk of the tree Peter stood in front of. It was not able to pull them out. With the Screamer unable to free itself, Peter turned to his teammates, who both had grins on their faces. They were impressed by his quick thinking. Peter proceeded to try to pet the creature. It didn't welcome his attempts to do so, however. Every attempt to pet it was met with fearsome teeth.

"I told you, Pete. No reasoning," JD said over the sound of snapping jaws.

"I've barely had a chance to do anything," he retorted while looking at the monster with a curious look.

"We don't have time for this," Damien put in. "We have a mission at hand that we need to accomplish. Silence the thing before it attracts any more of them."

"Okay," he said reluctantly as he dropped his head.

He pulled out his knife and prepared to make his next move. Knowing it would have to be quick and painless, he got in position for what he hoped would be an instant kill. Standing behind the thrashing creature, he lurched forward and grabbed the monster, rearing its head upward. Once he had it at its peak, in a mere second he shoved his knife with force through the lower jaw and up through the top of the head. The creature writhed around for a few seconds before going slack and Peter yanking his knife out. Blood leapt off the blade and splattered onto the tree as he quickly brought it back to his side. The area was finally quiet, emptied of fierce screams. The men departed promptly, leaving the dead creature, whose claws were still fixed on the tree's trunk.

The men moved for quite some time, and Damien wondered about their exact location. By using the map given to them by Frank, he discovered that their destination was approximately fifteen miles away.

"Let's take a break," he said.

Upon hearing this, JD set his stuff on the ground and sprinted away while looking left and right for hostiles. The sudden action had caused Damien to bring his weapon up and ready to fire.

"What's wrong?" Damien called with a loud whisper.

"Nature calls!" The response made Damien drop his head and sigh.

JD ran behind some bushes, and Damien wondered why he didn't bother telling him that he had to go so badly earlier. To teach him a lesson, he decided to play a simple prank. He hadn't played any pranks recently, due to his nervousness, but he decided that it was an opportune time. He picked up a small pebble on the ground and glanced at Peter, who nodded in approval of what he had in mind. He tossed the stone a few times in his hand before taking a firm grip and chucking it sideways with speed at a newly exposed bare cheek.

"What the hell!" JD harshly said under his breathing to avoid yelling as he used one hand to check for damage.

"What's the problem?" Damien asked, chuckling a bit. Peter was kneeling on the ground in silent laughter.

"You made me piss on myself!" he said as he glowered at them. "Not cool."

"Warm?"

"Shut up!"

"The smell will at least keep Prisoners away from us," Peter chortled.

Peter's remark seemed to have been true because the team didn't encounter any Prisoners for the next fourteen miles. However, Prisoners were very confusing when it came to their movements. Damien remembered being taught that at the beginning of the war when the base was established, the Prisoners had seemed nocturnal. Once the military had gotten used to that and devised strategies, the creatures seemed to change to the opposite. So to keep safe, the base and all of its inhabitants stayed on full alert at all times. Guards and even scouts were always rotated on duty in case of a surprise attack.

They soon reached a lush valley, which had their destination at its center, the facility Frank had mentioned to them. The facility seemed quite ancient, and the men immediately became aware of the presence of a few Screamers in the area as they scanned from a nearby ridge. They could have handled the Screamers with ease and gone in for extraction, but Damien and the others couldn't help but wonder why there were so few. The fact that they were all Screamers was also odd. In any case, they had to rescue the scientist, which the Prisoners might have come to believe was a valuable asset, if they were, in fact, intelligent. This assumes that the scientist is still alive, Damien thought. If the Prisoners had already disposed of him, they could be walking into some sort of trap.

"Let's observe the facility for a few hours before going in," Damien said in a hushed voice. "It's best not to go in blind."

The men agreed and proceeded to observe the area. While observing, Damien started a conversation about what everyone did the night before to pass the time.

"What did you two do last night when I left you in the lobby?"

"We did quite a bit," JD answered, busily scouting the area with his rifle and writing down the number of Screamers on a pad he had pulled out.

"It was pretty crazy, too," Peter added.

"That didn't answer my question. Give me some details," Damien sighed. JD was the first to begin.

"Well, once you left, I made my way to the closest arcade. I ended up spending about half of all of my money in there. Those games have to be rigged. I felt hungry after that and looked for Peter. When I found him, we went to the food bar and ate almost half of everything on the menu. I'm surprised we ate that much to be honest. After eating, we partied a bit and came back to the room to sleep."

"All I have to say is, JD-6, women-214," Peter smirked.

"Whatever. What about you, Damien? Did anything interesting happen for you?"

Damien hesitated. Telling his teammates about meeting a girl from his past might get them going.

"Uh . . . well, once I left you two, I headed for the elevator. A girl came into the elevator with me while I was riding it to our floor."

"Oh!" Peter exclaimed, cupping his mouth. "What happened next?"

"Well, nothing really. I just stood there until she left. We said goodbye to each other though."

JD lowered his rifle and looked at Damien. The glare lasted a few seconds before he threw a handful of nearby sticks and leaves at him. He turned back to his observation after the surprise attack.

"What was that for?" Damien exclaimed in a low voice.

"You're stupid, aren't you? You were alone in an elevator with a girl, and you only managed to say bye?"

"Yeah, but it wasn't until she left that I realized who she was. I actually knew her."

"Wait, what?" JD questioned while turning his head from his sniper once more. A hand slowly started to reach for more leaves.

"No."

"What's her name?" JD asked.

"Moriah."

"Is that it?" Peter asked.

"I wanna know more about this past," JD glared. "We've all been best friends for a while. Why are we just now hearing about her?"

"Well," Damien began, "she and I stopped talking a long time ago. Her family is military, so she had to move away when they were re-stationed. We had been in a relationship at the time, but we were young, and I couldn't do the distance." A slight sadness had crossed his face.

"Well, it's looking like you may have another chance, bud," Peter said while drawing in the dirt with a stick. Damien squinted and still couldn't make out whatever it was. He took a moment to think about his teammate's words. He thought that perhaps he might have a second chance. The feeling alone made a smile rush to his face.

"You obviously want it," Peter added. "She had to have meant a lot to you. The past just wasn't the best time for you."

"Yeah," Damien replied as he let hopeful thoughts cloud his mind. "I did get to see her one more time after she left the elevator."

"Oh?" JD said while slightly adjusting to see better. "How was that?"

"Pretty great. It was just a short chat though. We started to catch up, but then she had to go due to orders she had for today. Afterward, we both decided to head to bed."

"Same beds?" JD swiftly asked.

"No, in different beds, in different rooms, and on different floors."

After that, Damien's teammates didn't seem as interested in his night. Both stopped asking questions. He decided to focus back on the mission.

"How many Screamers have you counted?" he asked as he moved to sit by JD.

"Fifteen. If we don't see any more soon, I say we go ahead and infiltrate. Let's get this mission over with."

"Sounds good." They waited nearly twenty more minutes, silently scouting the area.

"All right. Go ahead and start popping some, JD. Pete and I will make our way down there. Headsets on."

"Got it."

While Damien and Peter moved toward the facility, JD immediately started taking care of the Screamers. He counted each kill, and Damien could hear him over the earpiece he had put on.

"Uno . . . dos . . . tres . . . cuatro . . . cinco . . . cinco . . . cinco . . . uh . . . eight . . . nine."

"You know, I can teach you some Spanish when we get back," Peter said while he charged forward.

"Shut it."

Damien switched his rifle's fire rate to that of a machine gun, aimed, and fired at one of the remaining Screamers that had spotted him and was sprinting toward him. The kill was fast, with a short, controlled burst, and the feel of his weapon was amazing. He couldn't help but crack a smile at the power he held in his hands.

Peter was covering him, shotgun in hand. Suddenly, a Screamer appeared, lunging at Peter. A series of bullets silently left Damien's rifle, hitting the Screamer's body and causing it to crumple over.

"I had that one!"

"Catching it with your face is not recommended."

"It's really not," JD piped up. "Serious injury may occur and, in some cases, death."

"Well, now you can shut it," Peter retorted.

Both continued toward the facility. This time Peter managed to dodge a Screamer, snapping its neck and knifing the back of its skull as a counterattack. JD then gave an update that only four visible hostiles remained.

A wave of three Screamers leaped high into the air at Damien, who was leading the charge. He managed to dispose of two of the airborne beasts with his weapon. The remaining one rained down upon him with claws ready to rip him apart. As it was about to make contact, it was suddenly shot and killed by a far-off shot. Its body hit the ground, head mangled beyond recognition. Damien continued forward as he shoved his knife back into its sheath, with Peter behind him.

"One left," JD said in both of their ears. "No visual. Watch your corners."

The two reached the facility, and upon reaching it, they both noticed blood and bones on its steps, walls, and door. It must be the remains of soldiers, Damein thought. He wondered whether the way the kills were spread about was perhaps a warning or part of a ritual. Both thoughts sickened him.

As he walked toward the door, Damien signaled to Peter to break down the door and take care of business. While Damien stood to watch the front of the building, Peter rushed and slammed the door down, breaking it off its hinges. Upon entering, he caught sight of two unaccounted for Screamers. He raised his shotgun and killed both quickly without a second thought. Darting his eyes to a corner, he noticed a third one and raised his sights on it. It was backed into the corner. It watched Peter, seemingly looking for an opening to strike.

"Put your hands in the air, and face the wall!"

Damien turned to look inside from the front and noticed the Screamer Peter had cornered. It didn't heed Peter's command and rushed at him. Two swift shots were fired and entered the beast's chest, causing it to fall back into the corner and die. Once it was killed, Peter gave Damien the okay to come inside. Damien switched on a flashlight on his weapon's side and searched the large room. The room was surprisingly mundane. The height of the doorway, for example, was what one would expect a normal person to walk through. The entire layout was something you wouldn't expect those bizarre beasts to create.

They continued their search, and Damien came across a staircase that went straight down into darkness. The ominous pathway gave Damien pause. He was hesitant to move forward. While maneuvering his flashlight, something caught his eye. There was something on the steps ahead of him. He cautiously made his way down and picked it up. Inspecting it, he realized it was some sort of identification tag. Its design wasn't anything the military used, however. Perhaps it was personally made, he thought. It was old and rusted, with faint carvings on it. He put the tag in his pocket and continued searching, hoping to find the scientist. Peter didn't have much luck in his search either. It wasn't until Damien reached the far back corner that he found a body. It was a man, lying lifeless in the corner. The body was riddled with lacerations. Damien saw that the corpse's coat had letters on the top right, the place where a name is usually sewn. It was partially shredded though, and Damien had to use his hands to connect the shreds of cloth together. There was indeed a name, and "Dr. Wright" was written.

"Peter," his voice was one of disappointment, "I found him."

"From the sounds of that, I take it we're not bringing him back," JD said over the earpiece.

Peter raced to the scene. Since the scientist was dead, the men had to retrieve his belongings. It didn't take long to find them. They were scattered a few feet away from him. The men decided to search the body for any belongings as well. Damien was able to find the man's wallet. As he pulled it out, his hand slipped, and the wallet dropped open on the ground. His heart sank. In the wallet was a small portrait of a happy, smiling family. He then noticed writing on it that read "Home 09/27/21!!!." The man was scheduled to go home on the same day the team found him. He closed the wallet and handed it to Peter for him to put in the bag.

Damien went ahead to the front entrance to clear his head while Peter was still packing the belongings. The nametag was in his hands. He attempted to decipher the writing. The writing resembled English, but the way it was written was very peculiar. He wasn't sure, but it seemed like the name "Sarah" was on the tag. Suddenly, an outburst of screeching was heard in the distance. The sound was coming from the back of the facility, and it sounded like a large horde of Prisoners.

"I think I know where the missing Screamer went!" JD called.

"Peter!" Damien yelled. "We have to go now!"

"Right! Let's go!" Peter replied, running past him.

As the two raced back to the ridge, another Screamer chased after them. It was close behind Peter, trying to bite at his legs, but it was taken care of by JD. He shot a near perfect headshot. When they reached JD upon the hill, the team hid themselves and observed the facility. The area was soon covered with Prisoners, both Screamers and Slashers. Slashers looked nastier than Screamers and were bigger. Their teeth were longer, and their snouts were shorter. Each of their forearms protruded claws, which were often crimson, stained with blood.

"Got a grenade?" Damien said, turning to Peter.

"How about six of them?" Peter replied gleefully.

While the Prisoners searched for the ones who intruded on their territory, the men used two nearby trees as a slingshot. A bag of grenades was placed at the center, and all of the pins were tied together. The bag was pulled back between the trees, poised for launch. Upon release, Damien held the string that was tied to the pins, and all came loose. The bag zipped through the air toward the Prisoner-infested valley. The team immediately retreated.

"What kind of grenades were those, Pete?" JD asked as he sprinted.

"Oh, you know. Just extra explosive incendiary ones. Large area damage."

Moments later, the sound of multiple explosions could be heard along with intense wailing. When the wailing came to an eventual stop, the team believed that their attack was largely successful. With their mission complete, the men headed back to the apartment complex. On their way back, they passed by the Prisoner Peter wanted as a pet. Its entire body was devoured. They wondered what had devoured it. It might have been a pack of fellow Prisoners or perhaps something bigger. It was indeterminate.

It was close to dark, but they eventually made it back to the main gate, which allowed them entrance after a quick scan. The team felt triumphant. All that was left was to deliver the belongings of the scientist and drop off their gear at the armory. After that, they would head for bed.

When they reached the armory, Damien turned and noticed both of his teammates were smiling. They felt as good as he did. Damien and JD went into the armory while Peter decided to stay outside. Frank was spotted cleaning a weapon at a desk in the back. He stopped what he was doing and approached them when he saw that they had come back. His amusing appearance briefly stirred their composure.

"Thanks for not bringing the other guy," Frank said, noticing that Peter was standing outside but still smiling through the window.

"No problem, sir. We've completed our mission. We regret to inform you that Dr. Wright was found dead. Here are his belongings."

"Good work," he said, grabbing Peter's backpack. "Place your weapons and gear on the table over there. You will be notified when you are needed again. Until then, you are dismissed."

The team left the armory and returned to the apartment complex. They were tired, and all Damien could do was think about his comfortable bed. When they entered the lobby, JD and Peter became energetic again and parted. Damien headed toward their room. He kept the name tag he found at the facility, and he didn't think it was worth mentioning to Frank. He went inside the elevator and had a faint hope of seeing Moriah, but she didn't show up. He made it to his room and went directly to bed, falling asleep almost immediately.

CHAPTER 3

Chilling on Base

Damien's eyes opened to see the ceiling of his apartment room. He was surprised that he wasn't awakened by his teammates during the night. Upon turning over, he saw that they were still asleep. JD used his blanket like a cocoon, and Peter was halfway off his bed. Damien chuckled at the sight and decided to get up and eat breakfast. Not wanting to wake his team, he quietly got out of bed and headed for the door.

As he left their room and headed for the elevator, he reflected on his team's performance the day prior. He was proud of his comrades, and he felt that they deserved to cut loose and relax. When he pressed the elevator button, he again thought of Moriah. He hoped he would be able to see her during the day. His team didn't have any orders for the time being, after all. The only foreseeable plans would be getting called and having their mission evaluation soon. After that, a new mission would more than likely be assigned.

The elevator reached the lobby, and Damien walked out to find that there were very few people around. The smell of delicious food came to him, and he was determined to get something to fill his stomach. He arrived at a breakfast bar, and multiple cooks were busily preparing dishes in the back. As he pulled out a chair and sat, he took notice of the menu that hung overhead.

"How may I help you?" asked a man behind the counter.

He was in formal cooking wear. There were no stains on his clothing, leading Damien to conclude that he just took orders. That or he was really careful while cooking.

"I'll have two pancakes, an order of bacon, scrambled eggs with cheese, and a glass of orange juice. Oh, and I'd like some peanut butter on my pancakes, if you have any."

"Certainly, sir. Your order will be ready soon. May I interest you in an appetizer?"

"What do you have?" he asked in curiosity.

"Our special appetizer for the day is specially seasoned fried lobster to dip in a vanilla bean infused honey mustard sauce." Just the sound of it made Damien's mouth water.

"It really doesn't go with the breakfast I ordered, but it sounds too amazing to pass up. I'll take it."

After writing down it down, the waiter left and gave the order to the cooks. While he was busy watching the cooks, someone sat right next to him.

"Do you always get up this early?"

To his surprise, it was Moriah. His heart rate rose instantly.

"Oh, ha-ha! Not all the time. I thought I might as well this morning since my team is still sleeping."

"Ah, so you're a team leader," she said, gazing at the SF5-3 patch on his shirt. "What's your team like?" He contemplated how exactly he could describe his team to her, but he knew that just wouldn't do.

"Hmm, how about I show you?"

"All right," she said hesitantly but with obvious curiosity. "How?"

Moriah was deeply intrigued by his suggestion, and he was delighted to see that. With a smile, he reached and grabbed her hand. A surge of memories went through him as he pulled her with him. The familiar touch brought a smile to them both.

"Follow me."

"What's the plan?" she laughed.

"Not letting them find us is the plan."

"I don't understand what you mean."

"You will."

The two headed for the elevator, hand in hand. He looked at her and smiled again. She instantly noticed and smiled back. It felt like they really hadn't been apart for years.

After reaching his floor, he brought her to his room door. He signaled for her to wait and quietly went into his room. JD and Peter were still sleeping. He went over to Peter and flipped him over on the floor; then he jumped on JD and smacked his face with a pillow. As Peter was trying to get up, Damien pushed JD on top of him.

"Try and find me!"

Damien dashed out of the room and grabbed Moriah's hand once more. She finally understood what he had in mind.

"Run!"

The two sprinted into the elevator, leaving JD and Peter behind, and waited for it to close. Just as it shut, Damien was able to see JD burst from the room.

"Dang it, Peter! He took the elevator. Run for the stairs!" Damien and Moriah listened as the two ran down the hallway.

"Wow! Do they always go along with things so quickly?"

"Pretty much. It can get pretty crazy sometimes. Let's see how long we can hide from them. How well do you know the place?"

"I know it pretty well. I've been here for about four months."

"Awesome. You should lead then."

"No problem."

Moriah tightened her grip on his hand and moved toward the elevator door. Once the doors opened, she darted outward and veered right. Damien noticed that JD and Peter entered the lobby on the opposite end, but they didn't seem to catch sight of him. Moriah led the two down a side hallway, leaving the lobby. After a few turns, they ended up outside of the building.

"Where to now?" Damien asked. They stopped behind a neatly trimmed bush, and Moriah proceeded to scan the nearby buildings.

"There," she said, pointing upward. "We're going to the top of that."

There was a small tower some distance away, and Moriah believed it to be a good place to hide. She let go of his hand and ran toward it, leaving Damien to chase behind. After some distance, Damien noticed how fast of a runner she was. He didn't remember her being nearly as fast. She may even be faster than him, he thought. In any case, there was probably a good distance between JD and Peter and himself. Although, his teammates excelled in these types of games, and he expected more of a challenge to start soon.

They eventually made it to the base of the tower, and Moriah went through the doors and into the main lobby. Damien took a moment to observe the building. It resembled a hotel, but it was much larger than the one he was staying in. It must be for high-ranking officers, seeing how nice it looked. Perhaps Avery was inside, he thought. The thought of running into him made Damien feel uneasy since he was running around with his daughter.

After Damien went inside, he saw that Moriah was waiting for him by the elevator. He looked behind himself to see if there was any sign of his teammates, and they were nowhere to be found. He went to Moriah, and they both went inside the elevator. She directed the elevator to go to the roof of the building.

"We are in an elevator together often," Moriah said.

She gave a big smile and held Damien's hand again, locking their fingers. She was enjoying herself, and Damien was happy that she was. The elevator doors opened, and they stepped out onto the rooftop. It looked like a simple rooftop. There weren't any antennas, air vents, etc. There were a few small benches, however, and the two sat down near the edge to look over the installation. The sky had its usual color, and it didn't seem that there was a sun on that day either. Damien saw his hotel, which was dwarfed by the one he was on now. Two dots could be seen running out of it, and he could only assume that it was his teammates. He chuckled and glanced at Moriah, who was still admiring their view.

"This place is really beautiful," she said. "It may have the Prisoners and a grungy sky, but it has its beauty. It reminds me of Earth."

Damien noticed its similarities to Earth also. For an alien planet, it reminded him a bit of home.

"Do we know why?"

"Well, the best guess is that there were Prisoners, which were much more intelligent than the ones we are familiar with, a long time ago. The portal to our world was probably built by them, but there aren't any signs of the Prisoners ever visiting our world. To be honest, we know very little."

"I'm sure we'll figure it out one day."

Damien looked out again over the city. Dark clouds were forming again on the horizon, and he wondered if it rained as it did at home. He felt Moriah place her head upon his shoulder.

"We should do this again sometime," she said with a sweet voice. "I've missed you. Honestly, I didn't think we would ever see each other again."

"Me either," he answered. "It had been so long I didn't even recognize you. Still beautiful as ever, though." He smiled and placed his head on hers. Her hair was soft and smooth against his cheek.

"If we're both free, how about we go on a date soon?"

"Sounds great. My team will receive another mission soon, so hopefully it will work out."

"You better stay safe," she said in a low voice after pausing for a moment.

"I will. I wouldn't miss the date for anything. Trust me."

"It's hard to promise what you can't control. I don't want to lose you, too."

"I'll be fine," he said while holding her tightly. It crossed his mind what she meant when she said "too," but he didn't want to possibly bring up a sad subject.

It was close to noon, and Damien was counting on his teammates to soon find them. Instead of finding another place to hide, he decided to stay put and learn more about how Moriah had been since they quit talking.

"So tell me about yourself."

"What would you like to know?"

"Why did you decide to join the military and come here?"

After a slight pause, she replied, "Well, if you remember, I wanted to be a dancer. I've always wanted to make a difference, too. Unfortunately, dancing wasn't going to pay the bills, and they just kept piling. As much as I didn't want to join, I knew it would be the best choice for me. I needed the money to get my life back on track. After graduating from the military, I was deployed here. How about you?"

"I also wanted to make a difference, and I joined when I found out about this world. Before that, I was a martial arts instructor. I joined a martial arts dojo when you left to get my mind off things, and it went from there. It didn't work out as planned, so I needed something to fall back on. This was it."

"Maybe we'll both be able to make a difference together," she said, smiling.

"Maybe." Damien noticed a pair of soft footsteps creeping closer from behind.

"Well done, guys," Damien said as he looked over his shoulder to find his team frozen in sneaking positions.

"Dang it, Peter! I told you to move quietly!"

"Me! You were the one he noticed. I was quieter than a feather falling into water."

Moriah and Damien turned to face the two, and his teammates glanced immediately at Moriah, who still held Damien's hand in hers.

"Is this the one you told us about?" JD asked as he crossed his arms and stood upright.

"Yes," Damien answered, smiling. He could feel his cheeks warm up and knew a red tint had to accompany the feeling.

"Oh? What did Damien say about me?" Moriah asked playfully.

JD smiled mischievously, and Damien was sure that he would take the opportunity to mess with him.

"Oh, nothing much. He just told us how you already knew each other and stuff. It wasn't exciting, so it bored Peter and me." JD watched to see how she'd react to what he said.

"It probably wasn't as boring as waiting for you two to find us," she said. "We were expecting a challenge, but we didn't even break a sweat."

"Well then," JD said, not knowing how to respond to her reply.

"I'm hungry," Peter interrupted. "Can we go get some lunch?"

"Sure," Damien said. "Where would you like to go?"

"To get food," Peter said bluntly.

"I know that. Where?"

"Any place with food."

"All right. We're going to the lobby."

The group went to the elevator, and on the descent through the building, Damien was surprised by how quiet his teammates were being. He had expected their usual behavior, but the thought occurred that maybe they decided to act calmly since Moriah was there. They reached the lobby and went outside. Damien kept his eyes on his teammates, unable to shake the feeling that they would attempt something soon.

The walk back to their hotel took considerably longer than the journey away from it. It was the return trip that made him realize how far they had run together. However, with Moriah's hand in his, he didn't mind the long walk. Just the feeling of having her fingers intertwined in his made everything else fade away. He and Moriah seemed to have the same feelings as they had before. The smile she had while they made their way through the streets showed Damien that she was just as happy as he was. The memory of their first end quickly flashed in his mind. The fault had been all his, but he was determined to never let her go no matter what it took.

The group finally reached the hotel and went inside to the lobby. Unlike in the morning, the lobby was much busier. There were crowds by the bars and recreational areas. Only one bar was open, so the group decided to eat there. The smell of food made them all hungry. It was then that Damien had the realization that he had never eaten his breakfast earlier that day. A small sadness swept through him as he remembered the description of the appetizer once more. As everyone took their seats, a waiter approached them with notepad in hand.

"How may I help you this afternoon?" the waiter said, smiling at everyone. He was a nicely dressed, overweight gentleman, with hair brushed to one side.

"I'd like food, and plenty of it," Peter announced, happy to finally be able to eat.

"I'm sure, sir. Anything in particular?"

"Surprise me," he answered.

"Will do," said the waiter as he jotted down the surprise order. "What about you, sir?" he turned and asked JD.

"I'll have the special."

"And for you two?" the waiter asked, smiling at Moriah and Damien. It took a few moments of looking over the menu and a few comments from Moriah before he could make up his mind.

"I'll have the steak with mashed potatoes, along with fried shrimp," he answered. He turned to Moriah, waiting to see what she would order.

"That actually sounds pretty good. I'll have the same."

"All right," the waiter said. "Your orders will be ready soon. What would you like to drink?"

"Water should be fine for all of us," Damien replied in a questioning tone as he looked at his team and Moriah. They all nodded in approval, and the waiter left the group for the kitchen from which many delicious aromas poured.

"So, Damien," JD began, "are you ready to party tonight?"

"Party?"

"Yeah, party. You haven't partied with us since we've got here."

"We've been here less than a week, bro."

"So what?"

"Sorry, no party for me tonight."

"You have a countdown timer or something? After a week, it goes off allowing you to party." Damien glared at him as he spoke.

"Fine. Peter and I will party like we've been doing then." JD got up to leave, his voice playfully offended, but then he remembered the reason they were there. "After we eat, of course."

"Why not go party with them, Damien?" Moriah asked.

"It's not my thing. I might do it occasionally, but I'd rather hang out with a small group of friends and relax. Besides, I want to spend more time with you." Moriah smiled back at his response.

"Sounds like a plan," she said. "What would you like to do for the rest of the day?"

"I don't know," he said, checking his watch. It was already two in the afternoon. "We'll probably take about an hour to eat and chill out. Then, while my teammates leave to party, I'll take you to the arcade rooms and defeat you in every game."

"You think you can beat me at every game, but you might want to think twice," she said, taking his words as a challenge.

"We'll see."

"Yes, we will see."

The food arrived, and everyone began eating. It was mostly quiet while they were enjoying every delicious bite, with a few comments from both JD and Peter, which caused Damien and Moriah to laugh. Everyone ate to their satisfaction.

"We're going to hit the arcade rooms," Damien announced. "Don't stay out too late, you two."

"And what if we do?" Peter asked.

"You won't get any cake for a week," he said. Peter put on a worried face and promptly nodded.

"Are you ready, Moriah?"

"To beat you in every game, you mean? Sure, let's go."

They went to the nearest arcade room, and once inside, Damien searched for a shooting game in which he believed he would excel. When he spotted one, he took Moriah to it. There were two wireless, plastic pistols on the sides of the machine. The objective of the game was to shoot all of the targets in the least amount of time.

"Ladies first."

"Nope, you go first."

"All right."

Damien grabbed a gun for himself and handed Moriah the other. He pressed a button to begin the first round and waited for targets to appear on the large screen in front of them. A timer of twenty seconds flashed at the top, and red targets immediately started popping up. He quickly scanned the screen and estimated that there were about thirty targets. "Go!" the game shouted, and Damien aimed and fired his gun at each target, both mobile and stationary, with high accuracy. He was able to hit every target in fifteen seconds, and once the game ended, he turned to Moriah, who had a congratulatory grin on her face. It was her turn now.

"Not bad," she said. "Hit the start button for me." She stepped up beside him and held up her gun.

"Good luck," he hugged her from behind.

"I won't need it." She smiled, with her concentration still on the screen. Though she was focused, she took a moment to place a hand on his before bringing her attention back to the screen.

The game shouted, "Go!" once more, and Moriah began shooting the targets. Damien's eyes widened at how fast she was hitting the targets. He didn't expect her to be so good. The game ended quickly, and she was able to hit all of the targets in a little over twelve seconds.

"So what do I win?" she said, pretending to blow smoke off the weapon's barrel.

"You win a rematch," he said, still looking at her performance displayed on the screen.

"Bring it," she replied, hitting the start button and tossing the weapon to Damien.

Damien was outdone two more times but managed to win one game. They soon played many of the other available games and spent hours enjoying themselves. Moriah was victorious in the majority of the games played, which taught him to never underestimate her again. He admired how good she was, and he hadn't had fun like that in quite a while. When they finished their last game, he glanced at his watch and realized how late it was.

"I guess we should be getting to our rooms," he said.

"I have to report in before I do. I had an amazing day, Damien. Thank you." The smile she gave Damien made him feel great. He found her quite amazing like he did years ago—probably even more so.

"Anytime," he said. They both gave each other a hug. As she started walking away she turned back to him.

"Don't forget about our date," he said to her. She came back and kissed him on the cheek.

"I won't. Maybe we'll see each other before then. I hope so anyway."

"Hopefully. You never know. Good night and sleep well."

"You, too."

With those final words, she left. Damien went to his room and went to bed. With a smile he couldn't wipe from his face, he soon fell asleep.

CHAPTER 4

The Nest

The sound of rain hitting the balcony window awakened Damien. This was the first time he had witnessed rain since coming to this world, and it was darker than the rain on his home world and poured down heavily. The sky was very dark as well, and the lights on the installation remained on, shining on the belly of the storm. A phone rang on a desk under the TV, and Damien moaned because he knew he had to get up and answer it. JD and Peter weren't going to budge. They were both lying in weird positions on their beds. He figured they'd had a good time the night before like he had. The phone rang again, and he picked it up. It was a message that concerned their recent mission.

"Team SF5-3, you are to report to headquarters for mission evaluation at 0830," the phone speaker said. "Due to the rain, a bus has been scheduled to arrive earlier at 0815. Your appearance is mandatory, and failure to comply will result in disciplinary action. Good day." The call ended.

"8:30?"

Damien was still tired. He glanced at the clock next to his bed and realized that it was 7:58. Surprise struck him quickly. The alarm clock hadn't gone off for some reason, so he and his teammates had to get ready and catch the bus in almost fifteen minutes. He hurried over to JD and Peter and gave each of them a smack on the face.

"Get up," he said while digging in a dresser for clothes. "We have to be out of here very soon."

"But sleep," JD groaned as he rubbed his face.

"If we don't make it on time, then they said they will take disciplinary action. That will more than likely be given by Major Avery." Those seemed to be the magic words. Both JD and Peter flung themselves out of bed at a surprising speed.

They all rushed to get ready; seconds ticked by. After they were all freshened up and dressed appropriately, they hurried out of their room and rode the elevator to the lobby. There were only a few minutes left. Once the elevator doors opened, the men ran out and nearly bumped into some people waiting for the elevator. Damien noticed Moriah sitting on a couch in the lobby, drinking something. He quickly weighed the thought of running to say hello while his teammates rushed outside. Breaking away from them, he jogged over to her and trusted that they would stall the bus for him.

"Hi," he said, sitting next to her.

"Oh, good morning," she said, smiling when she noticed it was him.

"I don't have much time to talk. The bus is probably waiting outside for me. My team was ordered to go to headquarters." The sound of a horn could be heard outside over the pouring rain.

"I understand. I have to be there soon as well. Maybe I could ride with you?"

"That'd be great," Damien exclaimed. "Are you ready to go?" His question felt pointless as he noticed that she was dressed in proper attire.

"I believe so," she said, laughing and getting up from her chair. "But I am taking this coffee with me."

"Good because we have to go," he said as he grabbed her hand and started leading her to the exit.

Damien ran outside and into the rain with Moriah in tow. The bus was in front, waiting for its last passenger. It was an old-looking bus in design, and greatly contrasted with everything else on the installation. He found it odd that such an ancient piece would be driving around in such an advanced base. The door opened for him, and he walked in with

Moriah behind him, her hand still locked with his. To his surprise, JD was in the driver's seat.

"Why are you in the driver's seat?" Damien asked worriedly.

He looked to the nearest set of seats and noticed that the actual bus driver was lying motionlessly. His uniform with the term "certified driver" on the pocket gave it away.

"What's going on here?" he asked, looking to JD.

"Hello, I'm Jeremiah Koffee, and I'll be your driver today. Be sure to take a seat, and don't ask any questions. Necessary actions were taken to prevent disciplinary actions."

"JD," Moriah snapped from behind Damien.

"Well, he wasn't going to wait for Damien, but we fixed the situation. Luckily, this thing's been retrofitted. There's an autopilot feature here, and I'll go ahead and select headquarters as our destination. Oh, and don't worry about the driver. He's merely unconscious." Damien dropped his head and shook it. Before saying another thing, he went and took a seat, and Moriah followed.

His teammates sometimes behaved quite unprofessionally outside of missions, and this situation was a clear example of that, Damien thought. They had been reprimanded multiple times for things like this. Regardless of whether he had any part in it or not, he was the team leader and had to keep his team under control. Rank demotions had even been threatened before if his team kept things up.

"Look," Damien said from behind JD, "I wouldn't have minded if you kept up an argument or something till I got out here, but making someone go unconscious is taking it too far."

"He made me go unconscious just yesterday!" Peter barked from the back.

"I don't mind it when he does it to you," Damien called back. "Plus you were out of line."

"What did he do?" Moriah whispered from his side.

"He laughed rudely at the appearance of Frank, the guy that runs one of the armories. Normally I wouldn't mind a little laughter, but he wouldn't stop."

"Sorry, Pete," Moriah yelled. "You deserved that one."

"I know."

The talking ceased most of the way except for Damien and Moriah talking to each other. They shared memories of their past until the bus made its way to headquarters, making Peter hit his head against a window as it came to a stop. To avoid backlash, Peter wrote a note and handed a fifty-dollar bill to the driver, who was starting to wake up.

"There, that should make up for it," Peter said, patting the driver's shoulder.

"No," the driver said while shaking his head. Peter pulled out another fifty. This persisted until the man accepted a three hundred-dollar bribe.

"Why didn't you simply give him the money before knocking him out?" Damien asked.

"That would have been better," the man groaned as he accepted the money, counting each bill.

"That's boring," Peter replied with a frown as he realized his loss in cash.

A thought occurred to Damien, and he turned to the driver in hopes of him answering it, "Why does the bus look like this? It seems like a really old model when everything else on the base is very new."

"Good question," the man said as he shoved the money into his pocket and proceeded to stand up. "When the portal was first opened, we didn't know much about how it functioned. So naturally, there were experiments. One of those was to see how big of an object we could fit into it. A bit unconventional, but we went and acquired this old bus and brought it underground. Then we drove it through. Since we already had it here and it was a pain to even get it to the portal, with it being underground and all, we decided to leave it here and make use of it. A few tweaks and upgrades, and she's a nice ride."

"Well then," Damien replied as he wondered how they even got the bus underground to the portal. He'd have to ask that question at a later time, as they were growing increasingly close to their deadline. "Thank you."

"Anytime," the man said as he assumed his position once more in the front seat and opened the door for the team.

The group finally got off the bus and stepped out into the headquarters' covered walkway. Lining each side of the walk were pillars that each had floating water above them like those at the armory. The only difference was that the water was in the shape of orbs that orbited each other instead of rings. The heavy raindrops falling from the sky gave each ball of floating water a slight glow when they hit. Damien was amazed by the sight. The four headed for the entrance, a dome archway with grid-like patterns. There wasn't an actual door, just an opening to enter. A strange light seemed to flow like water from the top of the opening to the bottom. As the team stepped through it, they felt as though they were stepping into a whole different world. Despite the open passageway, they could no longer hear the rain or feel the cold wind. They heard only the soft hum of computers and quiet conversation. There were multiple computers with various scientists tending to them.

"Hey, this place looks like the portal room back on Earth," JD said.

"Yeah," Peter said while looking around cautiously. "You don't think the scientist I messed with is here do you?" He quickly scanned the room, but the man was nowhere to be seen.

"This is where I have to leave," Moriah said suddenly. "I'll see you in a bit." She kissed Damien on the cheek and walked off before he could even react. He didn't know what that was about until he saw Avery disappear off in the distance. His heart pounded for a brief moment before he was able to regain himself.

Damien led the group to the opposite side of the area and saw a man in front of a door with both a fingerprint and retina scanner. He approached him and found that the man had been waiting for them.

"Hello. It's nice to see that you're on time for something," the man said, grinning. "But just barely."

"We're always on time," Damien replied, slightly annoyed. He looked at the man's name tag, which read Josiah. He was average-sized, about five and a half feet tall, and he had both brown hair and eyes. He looked to be in his mid-twenties and Damien felt a small surge of the same familiar feeling he had with Moriah.

"We know," he laughed. "Major Avery ordered us to mess with you since your arrival at the launch site."

"What?" was all Damien could respond with.

"Come on, Damien," Josiah began with a laugh, "I know it's been awhile, but did you forget all of us?" It took several seconds before Damien realized who he was talking to.

"Oh yeah, you're Moriah's brother," he responded awkwardly as he averted his eyes.

"Did the whole family enlist?" JD said as if he had read Damien's mind.

"Dad, Mom, Moriah, and I," he said. "All enlisted, over time of course, and stationed in the same place."

"Any aunts, uncles, or cousins we should know about?" JD glared.

"Nope, just us."

"Did Moriah know everyone was messing with me? I mean, your dad kicked me in the groin," Damien said.

"That one was probably more for breaking his daughter's heart than talking back," Josiah laughed.

Damien knew what he had done in the past. He remembered that even with the distance after Moriah had moved, she still wanted to be with him. However, he couldn't handle the distance. For a few months, he tried just to make her happy, but there was always one thing that got to him. He couldn't hold or protect her from a thousand miles away. Eventually he ended it, and they soon quit talking altogether. The pain of the nights she begged him to wait for things to get better echoed deep within in his mind and cut into his heart. He was so grateful for the second chance he was getting but didn't believe that he completely deserved it.

"Well, I'm actually here to take you into the next room, where I'll help brief you on your next mission. Please follow me."

Josiah turned to the door behind him and had it scan both his thumb and right eye, and, after a brief moment, it unlocked and swung open. Damien and the others followed behind and entered a white room that had a long table at its center. A monitor was positioned in front of it. Josiah motioned for them to be seated, and they promptly took their seats at one end of the table. Shortly thereafter, three people entered the room. The first was Moriah's father. Damien noticed that he was carrying a folder that likely had to be their mission evaluation. The second person, to Damien's surprise, was Moriah, who smiled at him as she entered the room. He recalled Moriah saying that they would see each other later, but he didn't expect it to be for the evaluation. He couldn't help but wonder if the meeting would even be mission related. With the whole family there, he felt like he was about to be roasted. He shifted in his seat nervously as he pushed the feeling aside.

The third person was someone he and the others hadn't met. He was a blond man dressed in a lab coat. The whiteness of his lab coat matched the whiteness of the room, thereby giving the illusion that his head was floating. JD and Peter chuckled a bit at the sight, but he didn't take notice of it. All three individuals took their seats at the table, across from Damien and his teammates. Damien assumed that Avery was probably the highest ranked person in the room, and no one spoke before he did. Soon, he opened the folder and began reading its contents to himself. After he finished reading the documents within the folder, he spoke.

"Captain Rivers, you were sent on a mission yesterday to rescue Dr. Wright from a facility occupied by Prisoners. You were to bring back his belongings if he was found dead. In addition to disposing of a significant number of Prisoners, you have successfully completed the mission. You have been told that the portal that leads to this world will remain open for another two years; however, that may not be the case any longer. Dr. Wright was one of our leading researchers, and he had a journal that contained a great deal of research data. The journal in question was among the belongings you've retrieved. Upon inspection, his journal spoke about a possible means of closing the portal, a special type of key, which is located somewhere on this planet. His journal does not provide any location for the key, so we are at a dead end until we acquire more information."

The news intrigued the team. The thought that the portal would close within a couple of years had been with them for quite some time, and the idea of the portal potentially closing years before schedule was quite surprising. Avery continued his speech.

"Recently we have discovered a Prisoner nest, and there may be clues about the location of this special key there. It is approximately ninety-three miles north of here. We intend to send a few of our research scientists there to investigate, and your mission is to accompany them and provide security. You will travel by air, and land in a safe area that is about five miles away from the nest. You will be accompanied by two squads, one led by Moriah Dura and the other by Josiah Dura. Stealth is essential. Are there any questions?"

"How much hostility should we expect, and what will be our method of escape?" Damien asked. Infiltrating an actual nest seemed very absurd to him.

"Right. We're busting into their hood to snoop around. There ought to be a pretty good escape plan," Peter remarked and was met with a glare from Avery that stopped any more words from coming out of his mouth.

"You are to return to your point of landing. Helicopters will be standing by with adequate cover fire."

"All right," Damien said. "When do we begin the mission?" He decided not to question his safety. He knew that he had to have some amount of trust in the decisions of his superiors and the skill of his team.

"Your mission begins now. Josiah will lead you."

Avery stood and indicated to Josiah that it was the end of the briefing. Josiah walked and stood next to a door. Avery, Moriah, and the man in the lab coat proceeded to leave the room. Damien noticed that Moriah didn't utter a word during the briefing and wondered if there was anything on her mind. He was excited about being on a mission with her. After everyone else left the room, Josiah told the team to follow him. As they followed him down a hallway, he informed them of their equipment.

"You will have the same equipment you had on your last mission. You will also be given long-range communication headsets to replace the ones you used on your last mission. Also, on the chopper are night vision goggles. Might wanna use them."

The men stopped at an exit door at the end of the hallway, and rain could be heard pouring on the other side of it. Josiah gave each of them their headsets.

"The helicopters outside, and you should go into the middle one. You'll find your gear inside. I'll see you at the landing zone. Oh, and there is one problem." He opened his door, and Damien instantly became confused. "It's nighttime."

"I don't understand," Damien spoke loudly over the roar of the rain. "It was just daylight just a little while ago, and it's not even past noon."

"We don't understand either. This planet is starting to act strangely. You've noticed the sky has been orange? It was blue with white clouds a few months before you got here. We'll discuss it later. Mission time!"

It was raining much harder than it had been earlier. Josiah ran to the helicopter that was to the right of their helicopter. Damien and his teammates didn't bother to run because they figured they were inevitably going to get drenched. As they walked to their helicopter, Damien looked at the sky and saw lightning. The first few strikes looked normal, but eventually, the lightning started behaving strangely. Lightning stretched across the sky in a broken, grid-like pattern and pulsed a few times before it disappeared. It happened so quickly that he thought he may have imagined it, but he saw it happen again. Soon after the lightning started, the rain began doing something strange as well. When a drop would hit the ground, it would give off a glow then fade away. With thousands upon thousands doing that at once, it was a beautiful sight that lit up the entire landscape.

Once the team boarded their helicopter, the pilot informed them of the location of their gear and told them to sit down once they'd suited up. He said it was going to be a bumpy ride. The engines flared, and the blades started spinning. A moment later, the machine lifted off and headed toward their destination. The team put on their headsets and were prepared for the mission. Damien could hear JD humming songs from his favorite TV shows, and Peter attempted to beatbox to his humming.

As they flew through the air, Damien looked out at the landscape through a window. Everything had a faint glow from the pounding rain but not enough to see everything clearly. He remembered that Josiah said they would have goggles for seeing in the darkness. After searching, he located them under his seat in a small container. There were only enough for his team. He passed them along to his teammates and activated his own. All of his surroundings lit up brilliantly. Everything was much easier to see. He was able to see the rain and landscapes even more clearly as they soared in the sky.

As he observed the heavy rain, he remembered that an average helicopter shouldn't be flown in storms like this. As if his mind had been read, the pilot mentioned that the aircraft was specially crafted to withstand powerful storms many times stronger than the one they were experiencing then. He also mentioned that any turbulence felt would be minimal. Damien realized that the pilot must have been messing around when he talked about a bumpy ride. He was reassured, but his feelings of reassurance were interrupted by a voice that came through their headsets.

"We have ten minutes until touchdown. Get ready."

It was Moriah's voice. It had a very professional tone, and it was the first time Damien heard her speak so seriously. She continued to speak.

"Let's try to complete this mission ASAP. I am sure no one wishes to spend a considerable amount of time on a mission. Besides, I may have date plans later."

"Does Dad know?" Josiah interrupted.

"It doesn't matter. I can see and talk to who I want."

"Is he worth it after what he did?"

"We were young, Josiah. You and Dad need to realize that."

"Yeah!" some random soldier said in the background.

Damien felt uncomfortable as the argument when on. He wondered how often he had been a topic of discussion in Moriah's family. There was one more thing to be said by her.

"Whatever happens between Damien and me is between us." Her voice calmed. "I still like him, and he likes me. We got this."

"Winner!" the same soldier announced.

The last remark by Moriah was facetious, and Damien smiled. The helicopter finally reached its destination, and the pilot told the team to jump. "Touchdown! Go! Go! Go!" he yelled.

The doors slid open, and the team immediately jumped out. Water splashed under their boots as they hit the ground, and the rain was heavier than ever. Lightning continued to behave strangely as it flashed across the sky. The team was about five miles away from the nest, and Damien turned on navigation mode within his goggles, which was supported by the overhead helicopters. They had marked the destination in the database when they were at a higher altitude, and they continued to transmit data as they hovered above extraction. A blue dot was displayed with accompanying text that read "5 mi." He scanned the area to determine whether or not there were any hostiles close by. There were none in the immediate vicinity as far as he could tell. Their arrival was fortunately not anticipated by the Prisoners. With their territorial nature, the Prisoners would have surely come to attack them by that point. Damien's team soon met up with the two squads on the edge of the forest and discussed movement formation. It was decided that his team would be the one to take point. It suited him because he preferred getting the first action. He pulled out his pistol and led the way.

Though the group traveled four miles toward the nest, they did not come into contact with any Prisoners. The shrieks of Screamers could be heard faintly in the distance, however. The rain didn't let up, and streams and gullies formed, cutting deep into the landscape, making the area dangerous to walk around in. One wrong step and someone could sink deeply into the mud or be washed away.

With less than one mile left to reach the nest, Damien became uneasy from the lack of interaction with any Prisoner. There was bound to be several of them at the nest, yet none was around. He pondered if the nest had possibly been abandoned. The group continued to move, and the nest finally came into sight. There continued to be no sign of any Prisoner, but the group proceeded to tread cautiously, hiding in the vegetation that covered the forest floor. Damien and the others had expected the place to be crawling with them.

Upon reaching the entrance to the nest, which was a dark hole on the side with broken cement and metal jutting out of its edges as if a building was underneath, Damien ordered that there be ten guards at the entrance and another five circling the perimeter. The place was very large and dark, and human remains were scattered everywhere, possibly from a previous battle or even a hunt. The sight was unsettling and slightly frightening to him. It meant that the nest hadn't been abandoned but just left temporarily.

"We have to make this quick," he announced to everyone. "These remains seem to be somewhat fresh. Whatever is here will be back soon or may very well be in the facility somewhere. I don't want to take any chances. Let's get this done." He looked to Josiah for approval.

"You heard him," Josiah said with a pleased grin to Damien. "Move out."

Underneath the blood and bones was a smooth, reflective surface. The Prisoners seemed to have used this as a place to bring back their kills. The view was just as sickening as it had been at the facility during their previous mission. To avoid becoming victims themselves, Damien was determined to finish the job quickly. Josiah proceeded to take the lead and slowly made his way to the entrance, weapon drawn. He then signaled to Damien's team to throw a flash grenade inside and take out whatever may be inside. Damien acknowledged the order and peered inside. The inside was similar to the inside of the previous facility. He recalled Moriah saying that there was speculation regarding highly intelligent Prisoners existing in the past. Perhaps the nest was something built by them quite some time before.

Damien's team tossed three flash grenades inside, and once the flash went off, they rushed inside, checking every corner. After clearing the room, with still no sign of hostiles, they signaled Josiah to follow. The accompanying scientists were the first to come inside.

"Stay in here while we clear other rooms," Damien said to them.

He used his night vision goggles and found four separate doorways as others began to set up lights for research.

"JD, you take the door on the right. Peter, you take the left. I'll take center right, and Josiah will take center left."

Each nodded and went to their assigned door. Damien leaned against the outside of his door and peeked inside. It was a smaller room, and it had a hallway at the far end. He tossed in another flash grenade and waited. A bursting light flooded the area before it faded. He then went inside and checked each corner. Again, nothing was found, making the area safe. As he went to inform the others that the room was safe, there was a sudden, sharp pain in the back of his head. His vision became blurry, and he immediately lost consciousness.

His eyes slowly opened, and after regaining visual focus, he realized that he was tied to a chair in a different room. The technology inside the room was highly advanced and reminiscent of the portal's technology. A column was in the center of the dimly lit room, and several parts of it moved and flickered with different lights. There was a large screen with controls on the column, which made it all seem wildly complicated. A humanoid figure, whose face could not be seen, was standing in front of the column. It was wearing a black cloak of some kind, and the cloak exhibited pulsing green lines designed in grid-like patterns. It was wearing a black cloak of some kind, with pulsing green lines running in grid-like patterns all over it, similar to the lightning he saw on their trip there. Damien looked to the floor and noticed that there were multiple corpses, and he surmised that the figure must have been responsible for it. He could meet the same end, and instantly became fearful as the cloaked figure slowly began approaching him. He struggled to free himself, but he was unsuccessful.

"You are wasting your energy, Rivers," the figure said in a deep, chilling voice, with an eerie calmness. Damien froze. The being had known his name.

"You cannot free yourself. I have made sure of that. Once I am finished here, your comrades will have to come free you. However, will they be able do so before my brothers return from the hunt? Care to wager? Feeding an entire nest is quite difficult, and the hunts often do not completely satiate them. Many will still be hungry once they've returned, you see. I am here to talk to you, to give you the information you earnestly seek. You wish to know about the key to the portal, correct?"

"How do you know that?" he asked. The mention of the key surprised Damien, and he did not completely understand why the figure wished to provide information regarding it. He was unsure of its true intentions and was naturally hesitant in trusting it. The figure walked away from him and approached the screen.

"I am what you have come to call a Prisoner, a member of a breed whose existence you may deem unnatural. We were created by an ancient race that tried to play God. Our purpose was to be a class of perfect warriors—to fight their wars for them. However, they soon realized that they had crafted their own destruction. I am well aware of your world, and my kind will surely thrive there. You see, I've been studying it. Your kind has been oh so careless. Since the very second that portal was made even the slightest bit operational, it started sending information from surrounding machines into the interface of this planet. I had been monitoring and noticed immediately. Once I gained access, I studied all I could. I now know your languages, your history, your tactics. Everything. I've even completed global computer integration with all your information. That's why you can read whatever comes up on these screens, any screens on this planet, for that matter. You speak the language and that is what will display. This technology is far beyond your race. At least now it is."

"Why would you do that?" Damien choked as he tried struggling once more.

"It doesn't matter why. What matters is how we get to your world. There are many of your kind for us to feed upon and even enslave. Resources are scarce here, and it is not unusual for us to devour each other. We have grown tired of this. We have been living this way for far too long. Your kind has been waging war with us for quite some time now, but the real war will soon begin. Look at the screen. What do you see?"

The Prisoner pointed at the screen, and Damien's eyes followed. The screen displayed the landscape of the world. There looked to be many pillars, and a picture was beside one of them. It was a giant tower with vines growing up the sides.

"Giant towers," Damien replied.

He noted that there was a very large tower at the opposite end of the world. One that stood above all the rest.

"They are not just giant towers. They are what I have come to call Nightmare Prisons. The worst of us are held there. Ninety-eight percent of these towers are still fully operational, effectively holding the nightmare within. Your kind has combated many of my brothers, but everything you have experienced is nothing compared to them. You've had it easy. These are the ones who are responsible for the demise of our creators. They are truly horrific. There are two hundred Nightmare Prisons, and this button is one I created to unlock twenty-five of them. Releasing all would be a slaughter and wouldn't make things go as well as I plan. Can't have that now can we?"

He pressed the button on the control panel, which glowed and flashed green afterward.

"We'll certainly meet again," he said. "The information for the key you seek is on the screen. Oh, and thanks for playing by my rules. I have things to prepare for, and you have a visitor. Till next time, I am the Alpha."

The Alpha soon disappeared, walking off and leaving Damien behind. Damien gazed at the screen, and warning displays popped up on it saying to close the portal due to a massive containment break. A golden key symbol flickered over what he assumed to be the largest Nightmare Prison, and he easily surmised that the key was located there. Suddenly, Moriah's voice could be heard, shouting his name. She was his visitor.

"I'm in here!" he yelled. After a few minutes, Moriah broke through the door to the room, with her gun at the ready. She cracked a glow stick and tossed it in the hallway behind her, then dropped another at her feet. After spotting Damien and searching the immediate area for hostiles, she ran over and freed him.

"Are you okay?" She wrapped her arms around him tightly.

"I think I know where the key is," he said weakly. He had been struggling for a while, and the initial loss of consciousness had zapped his strength.

"Really?" She pulled back and looked him in the eyes.

"Yes, and we need to get out of here. They'll soon be back from their hunt."

"Who?"

"The Prisoners."

Moriah's face showed deep concern. Based on the size of the nest, there was certainly a large number of Prisoners returning. She turned and saw the screen displaying the warning. She approached it, and the monitor shone brighter with each step she took. Once she stepped within range of it, a voice was emitted from it.

"One human detected. Safety protocol activated. Activating interdimensional teleportation sequence. This is the last available sequence. Shelter will power down post-sequence."

A beam suddenly came from the floor and ceiling, instantly lifting Moriah from the floor. Damien jolted himself from beside the chair and ran to her rescue. Time went in slow motion, and he heard her say something.

"I always loved you."

She disappeared before he could reach her. Before she disappeared, Damien saw the fear in her eyes. He was stunned. His heart was racing, and a tear rolled down his face and fell upon Moriah's dog tags, which were somehow left behind. JD suddenly came into the room immediately after and saw Damien on the floor, clutching her dog tags.

"Damien, we have to go now. A large number of Prisoners are coming back. We've been informed that they are within a few miles of here. We have to go now!"

"Moriah is gone!" he yelled. "We have to get her back!"

"What do you mean?" JD asked looking confused, but Damien's body showed the situation was urgent.

"She got too close and disappeared. She's gone, and I can't do anything."

JD didn't have time for sympathy. "If you don't live, you'll never be able to save her," he yelled. He honestly had no idea what was going on but knew he had to say what he could to get his friend out. "You didn't see her die did you?" Damien shook his head. "And we know this planet does crazy things. Get up and go now!" A lone Screamer burst through a wall, and JD shot it with pinpoint precision.

"I'm going to catch so much hell for this," JD mumbled under his breath as he positioned himself for a run.

Damien regained composure. Freaking out wasn't going to save her. He searched the room for his headset and found it on a nearby desk. He glanced at the screen again, and there was text that read "Transport successful. Status of the transported: Safe. Location: Saturn installation." It turned off soon after, and the room was darkened. He and JD left the room. JD briefed him on what was happening as they rushed to the entrance. The scientists and squads were already sent off to board the helicopters. He, JD, and Peter were the last ones to get going to the helicopters. JD set his sniper to rifle mode and prepared for what was outside the nest. Damien had to focus, and worry about Moriah later.

"Where's Peter?"

"I told him to go fix the Prisoners a little surprise."

"I think I know where the key is located."

"Really? Where?"

"I'll tell you everything once we get out of here."

The two returned to the main room and ran through the entrance, leaving the nest. Another Screamer was heard, and it was very close. While running, Damien saw that there was a horde of Prisoners on top of the nest. Both managed to get a good distance away from the nest before the first Prisoner gave chase on the ground.

Suddenly, there was a series of massive explosions, leaving the nest covered in flames. Prisoners flew left and right from the impact. Peter certainly didn't disappoint. Prisoners continued to chase after them, running over those that were severely injured. Peter's surprise gave them valuable time to put more distance between themselves and their pursuers.

Peter finally came into view, and Damien noticed that he had cleared out a large area with explosives. It was large enough for their helicopter to land, and as they entered the clearing, the helicopter landed. There were no casualties, but there was a single MIA. Damien was determined to change that.

The whole team boarded, with Peter greeting them with a nice "Howdy." As the helicopter lifted up, a new type of Prisoner called a Pulser, which the team hadn't yet encountered in the field, appeared. These types had the capacity of discharging energy from their hands, which resembled claws. The energy was produced by organic packs in their arms. They were very deadly and quite capable in both close- and long-range combat.

Soon, another type of Prisoner appeared that the team hadn't encountered before, a type that had come to be known as Giant Demons. Damien was told that they did not appear often, except in large-scale combat. Not much was known about them, but their appearance was hellish.

As the helicopter moved away, a green ball of energy arced through the air, launched by a Pulser. A tree was also ripped up from its roots and tossed into the air by the Giant Demon. Fortunately, the helicopter avoided the Prisoner's attempts to cause a fiery death. The tree fell back to the ground, and the fired energy created a crater when it impacted the ground. The impact caused a tremendous upward shockwave, which greatly disrupted the flight of the helicopter. Damien tried to hold onto something but hit his head against the interior. He was unconscious once again.

CHAPTER 5

A Change - JD

Night of Incident

JD's heart was pounding. He didn't know what was beyond the darkness in front of him, but he prepared himself mentally, looking toward his teammates as they all prepared to do the same. Damien was up against a wall beside his own door, with a flash grenade in hand. JD had one of his own and pulled the pin at the same time Damien pulled his. JD looked into the darkness as the cylinder of cold steel left his fingertips. The shadows were eliminated in an instant and he infiltrated the room, sweeping his light from wall to wall.

"Room is empty," he said through his mic.

"All clear," Peter announced over the headset.

"First area cleared," Josiah called. There was silence as they waited on Damien to report. The seconds ticked by without a word spoken.

"Damien," JD called. There was no response, and the seconds grew into a minute.

"JD, Peter," Josiah said urgently, "form up on Damien's location immediately."

Fear was like a knife slowly making its way deeper and deeper into JD's body. He rushed out of his room and immediately to Damien's last known location. There was nothing to be seen. Even as Josiah and Peter arrived to help with the search, nothing was found.

"You two find him," Josiah said quickly. "Stick together and watch each other's backs. I don't see any blood, so he had to be taken alive. Whatever took him has to be close. I'll carry on the current mission out here. Find him, execute hostiles, and get back here."

JD looked past him and into the concerned faces of onlookers. Not even five minutes into the compound and already an MIA. Then he saw fear he didn't expect to see. He saw Moriah's face. She seemed to be trying to work out what had happened and how. It had been so fast. Then she ran up to JD.

"I'm going," she said in a stern voice.

"No, you're not," her brother came back as he grabbed her. "I need you out here. Those two can handle themselves and find him."

"I have to help!"

"No, you don't, Ms. Dura. You will stay here and continue the mission, and that is an order!" There was a loud and crisp smack that echoed in the silence.

"Screw you and your orders," she said as she looked straight into the eyes of her brother. Her voice didn't waver, and her stance was solid. "I'm going, and you're not stopping me. I know you don't care for him because of the past, but he is everything to me. I never stopped caring, and I'll do anything for him." She spun around from the shocked face in front of her to meet the new shocked faces that were JD and Peter.

"Let's go," she said as she brought her weapon up and walked into the unknown. JD didn't know how to feel about anything, and he looked to Peter, whose mouth was slightly agape. He then turned to Josiah.

"Make sure she doesn't do anything stupid," Josiah said with anger in his voice. "I'll have a talk with her later."

"Yes, sir," JD turned and followed after Moriah, who had a slight lead. She was acting out of fear and anger, which he knew could get her killed. With a few strides he caught up to her and placed his hand on her shoulder. The motion was met with a flying hand that he dodged just in time.

"Whoa!" he said as he saw a tear glistening on her cheek.

"I can't lose him," she choked. "I always wished for another chance. To have what we couldn't have before. I finally got that wish, only to have it taken away." JD looked at her with sympathy. He couldn't feel the pain she was feeling, but he knew it was a pain that could be crippling.

"Look, everything is going to be okay. We'll find him. Just take it easy on your brother. He just wants you to be safe."

"You weren't there when he threatened Damien. He didn't want him to ever have a chance at coming back into my life. I forgive Damien. We were young and confused. We didn't know how life worked. Luckily, we were given a second chance to be with each other. I just want to keep that chance."

"You love him don't you?" JD smiled.

"Yes," she smiled back. "Very much so, and I want to tell him I never stopped."

"Then keep that smile because we'll find him in a little bit, and you can tell him. Deal?"

"Deal."

"Good." He turned to Peter. "Start cracking some glow sticks. Leave them as a trail so we can find our way back with ease." Peter followed without question and pulled out the first marker and lit it up. He tossed it to the floor, and the group began walking.

Minutes passed, and with each minute, JD felt more and more worried. He didn't know how things would be if the worst had happened. All he knew was that he had to think positive and focus on finding his friend. They soon came into an opening that held computer-like machines. It was then that an idea sparked.

"Take five and check out the area for clues. I'm going to mess with these computers and see if I can find some type of installation map or something." He looked down at the foreign controls and sighed. "Or something."

"I really think we should be searching rooms still," Moriah said as she scanned the floor for anything that may indicate that the hostile had run through.

"We will, but right now we have no lead as to where it went. So our best chance is to try and find a clue first before we blindly go searching." His words seemed to leave her in silence. He waited to see her begin searching again before he turned back to his foreign controls. "I have no clue what I'm doing, but I believe I've seen enough movies to figure it out." He pressed a button, and lights began flashing red repeatedly. Strange letters appeared on the screens that changed to show the word "WARNING." Quickly, he pressed the same button, and it all went away.

"Nope," he said as he looked around cautiously to see if his mistake had attracted anything. Moments passed and nothing appeared. Then an idea struck him. "Peter, the way back is clear. So ask Josiah if we can borrow one of the scientists who is proficient in this technology."

"Gotcha." Peter sprinted out of the room with his weapon at the ready.

"We're wasting our time," Moriah said angrily toward JD. "For all we know he could be in the next room, and we're worried about finding a map where there may be none."

"Look, Ms. Dura, we need to be calm and levelheaded. Trust me, I wish I could freak out right now but we're on a mission, and that's what we have to treat it as. We'll find him. Just be patient." She went silent once more as JD went back to looking at the controls. It wasn't long before Peter came back with a scientist.

"What do you need, sir?" he questioned as he approached JD.

"I need you to access this control panel and see if we can get a map of this place. With it, we may be able to find an area of interest to search for Captain Rivers."

"Yes, sir," the man responded as he took control of the foreign mess of tech. In mere moments, the lights appeared once more.

"I already tried that, even though I didn't know what I was doing."

"No, I knew what I was doing. This should not be happening."

"What do you mean?" JD asked with concern in his voice. Peter was right beside him.

"What's going on?"

"Something is causing a warning to come up. It's nothing I did. All I did was try to bring up a selection menu," the scientist said as he touched the controls. "Finding out what the warning is for right now."

"Tell me the second you find out," JD said as he focused on the screen.

"Oh, no." The fear in the man's voice was apparent.

"What? Why 'Oh no'? I don't want that."

"We have to evacuate. There are so many coming." With one last movement of his hand on the control, he brought up one more screen. On it was what appeared to be a distance countdown and camera views of a mass of approaching Prisoners. The sight was paralyzing for a moment before JD could regain his composure.

"Peter, take the man back now and tell Josiah. Tell him he needs to get everyone to the evac site right now. I need you to set explosives wherever you can. The moment you see the first Prisoner appear, I want you to blow them away."

"What about you?" Peter worriedly asked.

"I'm looking for him with what little time I have left. Even if you don't see me, I want you to blow this place up. Anything to take them out and get everyone away safe." Peter gave his friend an instant hug.

"See you soon," he said before he escorted the scientist out in a hurry.

"Now, Moriah," JD announced as he turned to an empty room. She wasn't there, just a glow stick she had left at the bottom of a doorway.

"Why?" he yelled, and sprinted to the first stick, only to find more making a pathway into the dark unknown. As he followed the trail, he wondered how long she had been gone. He didn't know how much of a head start she had on him. As he rounded a corner, he encountered a lone Screamer sniffing the ground. He couldn't stop his sprint without faltering, and he didn't want to take the chance of missing with his weapon while he sprinted. Instead, he brought out his knife, and the creature turned to take notice of him. A second before it was able to release its piercing scream, JD lodged his blade in its throat. The next second he used the weight of the target and his momentum to swing and bounce off a wall as he yanked the knife free. The creature's mouth gurgled as it spun around to try for its last attack, but JD had already launched the knife into the air. Impact occurred a moment later, and the sharply honed steel jutted from its cranium as it fell to the ground.

He went to the downed body, slid his knife out of the skull, and continued on his way. Corner after corner was turned with no more hostiles to be seen. Then something caused him to stop immediately. In front of him was a cloaked figure. Sporadic grid patterns pulsed all over. He didn't know what it was, but he knew all the friendlies were gone. Whatever was before him had to be hostile. The second it made a slight movement, JD launched his knife with astounding speed. The knife flew swiftly and with such deadly accuracy that he knew it would be a fatality. The figure had allowed him the first move. He knew that was its first and last mistake.

There was a flash of movement, and before JD knew it, the knife was sunk up to the hilt in the wall, the cloaked figure grasping the handle. The glow from a stick and the cloak itself showed a smile slowly spreading across a pale face.

"Nice try, Koffee." The voice was cold yet playful. "Maybe next time, but you better hurry. He doesn't have long." Before JD could bring up his weapon to fire, the figure was a blur, disappearing into the doorway lit by Moriah's glowing trail. He knew he couldn't pursue, but he was still in shock of what he had witnessed. Something had taken his hardest throw and caught it like it was nothing. Not only that, but it had buried the blade into the stone wall like a hot knife through butter. If it had decided to engage, he knew death would have been imminent. The thing even knew his name. His heart pounded as he continued onward with his growing fear of the darkness.

A minute later the glow sticks finally came to an end, and JD entered the room. He immediately saw Damien. He was on the floor near what seemed to be a computer system. Moriah was nowhere in sight, and JD knew that was not a good sign. She should have been there. He ran up to his friend.

"Damien, we have to go now. A large number of Prisoners are coming back. We've been informed that they are within a few miles of here. We have to go now!" His voice was slightly out of breath, and his nervousness was palpable. He had to get Damien out immediately. There was no more time to waste.

"Moriah is gone!" Damien burst out suddenly. "We have to get her back!"

"What do you mean?" JD asked. He was confused as to what he meant. At the moment, he didn't really care. He felt bad for Damien, but they would all be dead if they didn't go.

"She got too close and disappeared. She's gone and I can't do anything." Sorrow was heavy in his voice, but JD knew he didn't have the luxury of sitting and mourning. He had to do something to get Damien out of there.

"If you don't live, you'll never be able to save her," he yelled to pierce through the pain that shrouded Damien. He had no clue as to what had happened to Moriah, but he had to reassure Damien somehow. "You didn't see her die did you?" His friend shook his head in response. It was comforting just to see that he was listening. "And we know that this planet does crazy things. Get up and go now!" JD heard a cracking noise and drew his pistol. A moment later a Screamer burst through the wall, and he released a bullet into its head with dead-on precision. The creature hit the ground and moved no more.

"I'm going to catch so much hell for this," he mumbled under his breath as the possible repercussions from Josiah flashed through his mind.

JD looked down at his captain, who seemed to have regained his composure. He had stood up and gone to search for something. A moment later he grabbed his headset that had been lying on a nearby desk. JD wondered what all had happened in the room. It was then that he looked up at a looming monitor. What it said made him even more confused. There was readable text on the screen that indicated that something had just been transported to an installation on Saturn. JD instantly connected Moriah's disappearance to the text on the screen. He knew that had to be where she was.

The room darkened, and the two left, following the trail Moriah had left in her search for Damien. JD was leading the charge and would look back occasionally to make sure Damien was still there. He briefed him that there were countless Prisoners inbound and that the mission had been abandoned.

"Where's Peter?" Damien yelled over the sound of their feet slamming into the floor.

"I told him to go fix the Prisoners a little surprise."

"I think I know where the key is located," Damien said suddenly.

"Really? Where?" JD called back as he wondered how Damien could have possibly found that out.

"I'll tell you once we get out of here!"

Soon, they reached the main room in which they had entered when they first arrived. Everyone was gone, and JD looked for signs of Peter. Once they made it out of the building, Damien took the lead to the evac site. JD switched his sniper to rifle mode and prepared for battle.

As they cleared the building, a Screamer was heard close behind. The two looked over their shoulders to see that the horde was crawling all over the nest. Both managed to get a good distance away from the Prisoner before the first gave chase to them on the ground.

Suddenly, the forest around them lit up with a series of bright flashes as the nest blew apart and was engulfed in flames. Prisoners scattered like confetti from the explosion. Peter had certainly not disappointed with the surprise. However, even after the big explosion, the uninjured still gave chase. Many ran over the injured, but the whole ordeal had given JD and Damien more distance between themselves and certain death.

JD looked ahead, and Peter was in sight. There was a helicopter behind him. However, he wasn't at the evac site. He seemed to have cleared out a large area with explosives, a big enough area for the aircraft to land safely.

The three quickly boarded the aircraft, and Peter gave a "howdy" greeting. His smile was big from seeing his friends again. JD's smile vanished when he realized that Moriah was nowhere to be seen. JD knew he would have to break the news to Josiah when they were clear.

As the helicopter lifted off, a glowing green light caught his eye. Then more and more appeared, and his heart stopped. They were Pulsers. He had never encountered them in the field before, but he knew the damage they could cause. What followed was something that only elevated his level of fear even further. It was a Giant Demon. Just the look of it wrenched his gut.

Soon a Pulser fired the first arcing shot as the Giant Demon ripped a tree from its roots and threw it. The helicopter pilot must have seen the incoming projectiles as he quickly maneuvered to avoid them. Both impacted under the aircraft at the same time and sent a shockwave upward, bombarding the helicopter with wind and wooden shrapnel.

The machine jerked and turned. JD turned in time to see Damien slam his head into the side of the interior. His body went limp, and he started sliding out. Before JD could even make his move, Peter lurched into action. He caught Damien by the belt and lay flat on the floor as Damien dangled from the helicopter. JD quickly clipped Peter to a safety and then himself. Soon they pulled Damien onto the floor safely and clipped him in as well. JD checked for a pulse and was relieved to find out that Damien was only unconscious.

The helicopter had stabilized and was on a smooth flight home to base. JD finally had time to breathe. He looked over at Peter who was holding Damien still and wondered how all of it had gone all wrong. It was as though their arrival had been anticipated. Then he heard Josiah in his ear.

"JD, I need a status report," he said. "Moriah, are you okay?" The words pained JD. Josiah had assumed that she had made it back and was safe. JD let a moment tick by in silence before he spoke.

"We have Damien, but he was knocked out during take-off."

"That's good. I knew we would find him. Moriah, are you seriously not answering me because of earlier? Everything is fine now. I'm sorry, okay?" Silent static filled the headsets. "JD?"

"She disappeared somewhere in the facility." The words felt slow as they left his mouth. He looked to Peter, who was hearing everything for the first time.

"No, no, no," he said with a laugh. "I know you like to joke, but I really don't feel like playing. Tell my sister to answer me."

"She's not here, Josiah. She's MIA. She ran off on her own to find Damien, and when I found him, she was already gone. We didn't have time to do any searches, or we all would have died."

Then the rage burst through the mic. "I told you to look after her!"

"Sir, I did what I had to do." JD knew Josiah's rage was not going to wither anytime soon, so he turned off his headset and listened to the hum of the helicopter.

"So what all happened?" Peter asked as he sat on the floor with Damien.

"Too much," JD began. "After you left, I realized she had gone ahead, so I chased after her. I found one Screamer on the way and was able to kill it. Then . . ." He paused. He wasn't sure what to say about the figure that had caught a thrown knife like it had been nothing but a feather and slammed the blade all the way into the wall. Even the fact that it had known his name gave him chills. He decided not to mention it. "After following a trail Moriah left, I found Damien, but she was already gone. According to what was on a screen in the room, she is on an installation on Saturn."

"She's what?" Peter seemed confused.

"You heard me," JD said as he stared off into space, trying to wrap his mind around all that had happened. "Let's just try to rest until we get back. Call for a medic to pick Damien up upon landing. For now, I think I see a little blood on his head. Patch him up and keep him stable." There were no more words that were said on the flight back to base.

Soon the helicopter touched down, and a few medics were making their way to acquire Damien. There was another person also on the way from where he had landed, and JD knew it wasn't going to be good. As JD stepped off the aircraft, Josiah met him with a punch before he was restrained by other soldiers.

"How could you lose my sister?" he yelled. "You're no better than your captain!"

Fury grew inside of JD, but he just closed his eyes and turned away as he rubbed his jaw. "That hurt a bit," he said as he turned to Peter. He looked over his shoulder to see Josiah walking away. He knew fighting wouldn't solve anything, but he had to let his anger out on something, and JD let it be him.

"He'll calm down eventually," Peter said as he and JD followed behind the medics that had Damien. He had still not yet awoken, and they were both starting to worry.

"We'll see," JD said as he stared at Damien. "Let's just focus on Damien right now. He may have hit his head harder than we thought." Peter's face showed even more distress after JD's words. All he wanted was for everything to be okay.

They had made it into the hospital within five minutes, and JD and Peter were in the waiting room. Each minute that passed brought even more unease as their worry grew. After waiting for what had seemed like hours, a doctor finally walked up to them.

"He's currently in a concussion-induced coma from hitting his head. He could wake in a few hours, a few days, or a few weeks. It's just a waiting game. Would you like to go in and see him?"

"Yes, please," Peter said instantly as he got up from his seat. JD followed suit and stood with him.

"Right this way."

As they walked, JD didn't know what to think or feel. He had seen a figure that moved faster than anything he had seen before, Moriah had been sent to Saturn, and his friend was in a coma. He only wondered how

Peter was taking all of it. He looked to his friend and saw the worried expression on his face. He knew he couldn't tell him that everything was going to be okay because he himself had no idea.

Soon, they were standing in the same room as Damien. He was laid up in a hospital bed with monitors and other machines connected to him. It was a sight neither JD nor Peter wanted to see.

"I'll leave you alone for a bit," the doctor said as he stood at the door. "If he happens to wake up or move, make sure to notify someone immediately."

"Alright," JD said as he stared forward. The doctor left and the minutes passed, first one, then sixty. All he could do was wonder what he could have done differently to change things. He saw Peter out of the corner of his vision, and he seemed to be in the same deep thought. JD's thoughts, however, were starting to get to him.

"I really hope he wakes up soon," JD said as he looked straight ahead. His chin rested on his hands.

"Me, too," Peter responded in a mellow tone. "You think he is going to be okay?"

"Yeah, the doctor said there shouldn't be anything to worry about." He knew the doctor hadn't said those words exactly, but that is what he hoped. However, Peter didn't seem to be talking about that.

"I didn't mean it like that. I'm talking about Moriah. He seemed to really care about her. Don't really know their past, but they seemed close, and he lost her." The thought had occurred to JD. He knew the impact of the event would affect Damien hard. He had already broken down the moment he had lost her. JD was scared for his friend after the loss had had more time to sink in. In the meantime, he had to be hopeful.

"We'll be there for him to make things better. Plus, I was there moments after she was gone, and I saw some screen. Apparently she is safe somewhere on Saturn."

"Saturn?" Peter asked inquisitively. It may have been a small and innocent question, but it had sent a wave of annoyance through JD. He couldn't make sense of anything, and all the mysteries just kept piling up. He just wanted things to be simple.

"Look, Pete, this place is crazy, and I don't understand any of it much. I do know that we were sent here to do missions to help end this madness.

Maybe we'll find the answers in the meantime. But right now, I just want to relax and have what I can under control. You should do the same." The words had felt like a snap, and he knew his friend didn't deserve his impatience. Silence lingered between the two before JD left without a single word. He had to have time to himself.

Upon entering the hallway, he felt a pang of guilt. Peter was just trying to understand like he was. He also worried just as much about Damien.

"I'll make it up to him soon," JD told himself as he began his journey to his bed at the hotel. He believed that rest and time alone would do him well. Before he could even make it to the lobby, he let out a sigh. Avery was walking right toward him.

"Koffee," Avery said as he came within hearing distance.

"Yes, sir," JD responded with an unpleasant voice as he came to an abrupt stop and took his stance.

"Look, I know you just had a rough mission," he began. JD could see the red in his eyes from shedded sorrow. Still, even in the sadness, the man kept a stone-hard demeanor. "Josiah filled me in on most of it. However, I will need a full account from you. It doesn't have to be tonight. Just drop by my office sometime tomorrow to give the report." It was a bit comforting that Avery was being so understanding, but it also seemed strange. His daughter had just disappeared, and he was being nice. JD thought maybe there was more to Avery than he first thought.

"Yes, sir. Time?"

"Whenever is best for you, soldier," he said as he patted JD on the shoulder. "I will be in the office all day tomorrow. Lots of paperwork to file." With those final words, he walked past and disappeared around a corner. After he had left, JD wasted no time in continuing on his way out of the building.

Exiting the hospital somehow gave a bit of relief. It let him know that the night was done and that the fight was over for the moment. As he walked to the hotel, he tried to keep his mind silent. Thinking too much would bring about problems and questions. Instead, he enjoyed the breeze and the sounds around him. He looked upward and enjoyed the sky. It had its beauty.

The walk to the hotel seemed so short, and he was there in no time at all. The weight of the mission was starting to hit him. He realized that he was the most tired he had been in a long time. All he wanted to do was get into his bed and let the problems of the night fade away while he slept.

After a while of lying awake, darkness slowly started to engulf his mind, but then he heard the door open. He heard footsteps, but then there was a pause. He figured Peter must have been looking around the room. JD was too tired to muster a conversation, but he wanted to let his friend know he cared.

"Everything is going to be alright," JD said.

"I know, bud," Peter replied. With that, the two of them fell asleep.

CHAPTER 5.1

Someone New - JD

1 Day After Incident

His eyes slowly flickered open to show the ceiling above him. Light had barely started to stream in through the balcony's window. As he rolled onto his side, he saw that Peter was still asleep. It was really no surprise to him since Peter was normally the last to wake up except on certain occasions. JD, on the other hand, normally liked to get up and get things accomplished. He wasn't sure what his day would entail, but he knew the first thing on his agenda was going to talk to Avery. He took his time getting ready and tried his best to not wake Peter. It didn't take him long before he was down in the lobby getting his breakfast.

Thoughts swam in his mind as he waited for his food. The previous mission and all that had occurred. He didn't know what to make of all it. So much at once felt overwhelming.

I really hope you'll be okay when you wake up, he thought as Damien came to mind. He knew Moriah meant a lot to him. He saw the instant breakdown that brought his friend to tears. *We'll be here for you to help you out either way.*

As his thought finished, food was placed in front of him. He took a deep breath of the delicacies he had ordered. His mouth began to water, and he couldn't hold back any longer. Each bite felt like relief, like problems melted away with each mouthful.

"I'm gonna have to get this chef's number," JD mumbled to himself with a stuffed mouth. It took him a while to finish his meal, as he savored everything on the plate. When he had finished, he left the hotel and turned to walk to Avery's office but stopped. He looked in the direction of the hospital and smiled.

"I'll visit you first, bro."

As he walked, he relished the cool, crisp breeze that washed over his face. The warmth from an unknown source energized him. He started to feel really positive about the day. It wasn't long before he reached Damien's room and sat at the bedside of his friend.

"The fun we're going to have when you're all better is going to be insane," JD laughed. "Actually talked to one of your doctors on the way in, and he said it shouldn't be too long until you're up and going. He also said that due to some equipment they used, you'll have practically zero recovery time. Pretty crazy, huh?" Silence lingered in the air for many minutes. The hands on the clock seemed like they had spun quickly at one point.

"You know, we really miss you. I mean, my mood has shot down. I even started to push Peter away last night. I had to reevaluate myself a little. Everything should be fine now. I'll make things up to him even more. I'm sure he needs me, too, with you being gone right now. Please wake up soon?" With those words, JD smiled and left the room. He knew his friend was going to be okay, but seeing him lay there, almost lifeless, drained him. Turning his attention to the new task at hand, he walked out of the building and in the direction of Avery's office.

As JD was leaving the hospital, he stopped and looked around. He noticed all the other soldiers and personnel walking toward their own destinations. Everything seemed calm, but he knew the chaos that raged on inside each of them, the fear of safety and the sense of valor. The past days had changed his perspective. He was no longer an invincible, one-man army. He was only a single gear in a large machine. If a gear were to go missing, he'd have to perform as he always had and better to keep things going. He was a part of the machine of war and finally knew his place.

After taking time to reflect on his place in things, he set out for the office. It didn't take him long before he reached it. Upon entering, he saw Avery enter the lobby and immediately snapped to attention.

"At ease, Koffee," Avery said as he brought a cup of warm, dark liquid to his lips. "Follow me."

"Yes, sir," JD replied as he relaxed and followed his commanding officer. Moments later he was stepping into an office with a surprising object in it.

"What is that?" JD motioned toward it.

"If you have to ask, then I might question why I called you here," Avery said as he sat down and stared over his cup.

"Well, I know what it is, but can you tell me more of this particular piece?"

"Sure, it's the very first Prisoner I ever killed. Back in the portal room on Earth. I have it as a reminder that they attacked first and that they are merciless. When I see that, I know I wouldn't hesitate for a second to shoot it again."

"I see," JD said as he turned his gaze from the frozen creature and sat down in front of Avery. There was a moment of silence before Avery began speaking.

"How do you personally feel your first mission went?" His gaze was hard and unwavering.

"I honestly feel as though it could have gone better."

"How so? There were no casualties. Mission was completed with a good number of enemies taken out. Sounds pretty good to me."

"Yes, but we were a little careless. Not professional. We made time for jokes. A mission should only have time for the mission. That's what we're here for. The only time I personally found it acceptable was when we had to wait during surveillance. Even then we could have been perfecting the plan or scouting more."

"I see. And your second mission?"

"Even worse, sir. We were on too much of a high from the first. We thought we were invincible and that everything would be okay. We let our guard down more and were careless in our thinking. Had we had a different, more realistic perspective on things, I feel it would have gone better."

"I agree. Is there anything else?"

JD paused as an image of the cloaked man flashed in his mind. It was the first time he had thought of him since that night.

"During our last mission, I saw someone."

"What do you mean?" Avery's eyes widened at the words.

"When I gave chase to Ms. Dura, I encountered an unknown enemy. I believe he may have been the one who abducted Captain Rivers. He wore a hooded cloak with green lines across it. It's all a blur, though. That's all I can remember."

"Lieutenant Koffee, the information you know is confidential. You are not allowed to repeat it under any circumstance. However, in light of this information, I have decided to entrust you with a single-man mission."

JD sat in his seat and dared not move. He had no idea what was happening.

"I want you to make contact with the figure you saw that night. He is called the Alpha."

"How am I supposed to do that, sir?" The question came out slowly and confused.

"The next mission you receive will be soon, and your team will be traveling to the opposite side of the planet to acquire the key to shut the portal down. Along the way, he will, without a doubt, try to make contact with you. It is when he does this that I want you to gain his trust."

"Who is he?"

"He is the one who leads all of the Prisoners. If he gives an order, they follow. He has unimaginable physical strength and speed." With those words, JD remembered the knife he had thrown and how it had been diverted with ease. However, that no longer bothered him. The increasing suspicion in his mind was toward Avery. He wondered what all Avery really knew about the man and if he had ever actually talked to him. Curiosity won and spoke.

"Have you personally had contact with him, sir?"

"Yes," Avery responded without delay. "However, I have not received any information from him. I believe that with the coming events, he is going to make a big move. On your next mission, isolate yourself when everything seems safe. Whenever you're on watch. Just try and make contact. Show him you are wavering in loyalty to your race. Provide him a piece of information that only a traitor would give."

"Sir, you're asking me to commit treason," JD retorted, his voice calm but full of confusion.

"I know what I am asking you to do soldier," Avery snapped back. "The information you will be giving him is the information I am going to allow you to give. You will be acting as a loyal soldier in the eyes of the military."

JD took a minute to ponder all that was being said. He'd known it would be very risky, but that's was what was being asked of him. Those were orders he could not deny. He was only a single cog in the machine.

"What would you like to have me tell him, sir?" he said with confidence.

"I have a packet of information for you, along with the things I want you to say should certain topics come up. No one but you will see this. Is that clear?"

"Yes, sir."

After he had received the packet, Avery dismissed him, and he began his walk back to his hotel. Other than read over the contents of whatever resided in his orders, he had completely free plans for the day. He thought that he might try to see if Peter would hang out with him. After the way he had acted toward him the previous night, Peter deserved to have a fun day.

It didn't take him long to make his way back to the hotel and inside the lobby. Upon entering, he heard his name called from somewhere close, and the voice was vaguely familiar. He swept the room with his eyes and stopped when he found out where he had been called from. A tall woman with a svelte body sashayed up to him, her slender, elegant frame lending itself effortlessly to the walk. A shock of short, windblown hair sat ruffled on her head, raven black against her pale skin. Disbelief filled him briefly, but before he could allow it to empty enough to speak, she walked up to him and did it for him.

"Hey, did you ever open the note I gave you a while back?" she said as she smiled at him.

"Yes, and I'm pretty sure that I am not currently dreaming," he responded in a beyond confused voice.

"Well, you weren't as 'smooth and bold' as you thought you were, but you were cute. I know you really may not believe me, but I have the rest of the day free and was wanting to know if I could use it to prove myself to you."

It seemed too good to be true, and he was thinking very cautiously. He didn't want to get played and have his time wasted. As he looked into her eyes, he couldn't help but think that she was telling the truth. He couldn't even place the color of her eyes. He didn't know whether or not that was himself being hopeful, but he did know that the chance couldn't hurt.

"Sure, why not," he finally said, receiving an embrace soon after the words had left his mouth. Once she pulled away, he asked her what her plans were.

"I honestly didn't get that far. After rejecting you, I really didn't think you would have given me the chance."

"Well, it was a major offense, and you're now on probation. Let's see how you get out of it." His voice had turned into a playful one as a small wave of happiness went through him. It was a great feeling that he had not felt in a long time.

"How about we go get to know each other a bit? Maybe a walk?"

"That sounds great. I had thought of hanging out with my friend Peter, though. Really don't want to leave him out since he's probably going through some things."

"I think I know who you are talking about. The shorter one of you three? I saw him leave with Mr. Dura this morning. I believe they are hanging out today."

This was news to him, but he hadn't really talked to Peter since the mission. It was probably better that he was spending the day with Josiah. It gave him someone to have around, and Josiah probably needed a good friend to hold him up after losing his sister.

"Alright, then let our day begin," JD smiled. "But let me run this up to my room first. Wait here for me real fast?" She nodded her head, and he took off as fast as he could. It didn't take long before he was back. Once back, he asked if she was ready and motioned for her to take the lead.

"Yes," she said as she walked past him and grabbed his hand briefly then let go.

The two went outside and started to walk in a random direction. It wasn't long until JD started the first conversation.

"You know, I have no idea what your name is." He laughed. "Mind telling me?"

"Laurielle," she said. "I know yours, obviously, but if you want you can tell me again."

"Jerimiah Koffee," he responded with a grin.

"Smooth and bold right?"

"Yeah," he said as his cheeks turned red with embarrassment.

"That's a really horrible pickup line," she laughed as she playfully bumped into him. "I don't even know if I'd call it a pickup line. Has it ever worked?"

"Honestly, no." He couldn't remember a single time that it had caused anything other than rejection.

"Well, it may be horrible, but I found it to be kind of cute. So I guess you can say it worked on me."

JD smiled. "Good to know." He thought about how he would get to brag to Peter later on and tell him to add a tally to his name. Then the thought of Damien came into his mind and how he wanted to tell him, but he knew he couldn't. As he thought, he realized he had been quiet for a few minutes and that a small bit of sorrow had crept into his face.

"Are you okay?" Laurielle stopped and looked him in the eyes. He instantly averted his eyes from hers, but they soon found their way back. There was something about her eyes that brought him back. He wasn't sure if it was the beauty or the comfort they gave him.

"Sorry, I've just been going through a lot the past few days. Now even more is going to happen, and I know it's my duty to do it. Just don't know if I can even though I have to. What if I fail?" He felt his emotions on the verge of spilling over and knew he had to hold himself. Also, he had just met the woman and didn't want her to have to deal with all of that. He wanted her to want to stay around and not be run off. "Sorry again, I shouldn't have—"

"Shouldn't have what?" she interrupted. "Told me how you feel? Told me that you have your own fears but push them aside to show your strength?"

"We're in a time of war, I can't afford to—"

"Be human?" she smiled. "Look, I know we really don't know each other, but I want us to get to where we can trust each other, to where we can tell each other whatever is on our minds. I want to know you."

All of what he was hearing seemed too good to be true. He had someone in front of him, albeit a stranger, that cared for him and was wanting to give him the chance he had long craved for. Everyone starts out as a stranger. It's the bond over time and effort that decides what they become.

"Thank you," he said, then paused as though he was at a loss for words. "It means a lot, and I really want to get to know you as well."

"Then let us," she said as she reached for his arm and held it.

They began their walk forward once more, and conversations of their past sprung forward. JD told her of his childhood and how he had grown up poor. He had always looked forward to becoming something great. When he was younger, he had always looked up to those that were in the military and aspired to be like them. He made sure he was the best he could be before he even entered. Besides growing up wanting to be in the military, he had a loving family, but his love life was always like a desert, and he desperately searched for an oasis. Having never found it, he fell into the habit of trying to act as a player when approaching women. There were the occasional few that gave him a chance, but they never ended well.

When it was Laurielle's turn, she told him of a dark past, of how she grew up in the shadows and was lost. She never really had a family and almost had been to a point in her life where she was starving to death. It was then that a stranger she later considered her father took her in. He brought her up and taught her everything she knew. She told JD that she had no time for relationships growing up and was never in a good enough condition to be in one until a few years ago. She decided to finally start branching out and making something of herself, becoming someone her father would be proud of. JD found her story to be a sad yet beautiful one of redemption.

"Well, you seem pretty amazing, so you must be making him proud," he smiled at her. The joy in her face from what he had said was apparent.

"Thank you, that means a lot." She pulled him close for an embrace and then released. "How about I show you around the installation? It feels nice out, and I'd love to talk more."

"That sounds great!" All he wanted to do was spend more time with her and get to know each other better. For a while, she had made him forget about all of his trouble, and that was all he could ask for.

The rest of the day was spent casually talking and doing miscellaneous activities. As it drew to a close, they had made their way back to the hotel and were preparing to part for the night. Both had large smiles on their faces and were more content than they had been in a long time. JD reached in for a hug to say goodbye, but before he could react, she gave him a quick peck on the cheek.

"Thank you for the amazing day," she said as she then gave him a strong embrace. "I really needed it."

"So did I," he responded in a soft voice as he wrapped his arms around her and let his cheek rest on the top of her head. The moment seemed to last forever, and it was the most amazing feeling he had ever felt. Soon, they released each other and went their separate ways with future plans swirling about their thoughts. JD had given her his cell number so she could reach him in the near future. He had told her that he would be leaving on a mission soon and that it would be an extremely dangerous one. She seemed to be confident that he would be perfectly fine, and he didn't want to tell her otherwise. He knew positivity was what she needed.

He eventually made his way up to his room. The day had made him tired, but it was also one of the best. His mood was at a high, and he felt great. As he stepped off the elevator, he saw his friend in front of their room.

"Hey, Pete!" JD called out from the elevator with an apparent happy tone. He saw the genuinely confused look on Peter as he started toward him. JD could only guess that it was because the last time Peter saw him he wasn't very upbeat, and at that moment he was all smiles.

JD talked with Peter about all that had been happening to him and how he had met someone. He was happy that he and his friend were talking like everything was fine once more. The two spent the last few minutes before bed catching each other up on events before they fell asleep.

CHAPTER 5.2

Growth - JD

2 Days After Incident

Once again, JD had awakened before Peter and had left to start his day. He wanted to go see Laurielle, but she was stationed through the portal at the time. The next best thing he thought he could do was to go to the armory to see if Frank knew anything about their next mission. If he could prepare in any way, then he was going to do so.

The walk to the armory was a refreshing one. The wind was cool and blew against his face. It brought back memories of when he was younger, when he would stand in a field near his house and fly a kite high in the sky. He loved who he had become and what he did, but he couldn't help but wish to be back to a time of ease and innocence.

As he finally approached the armory, he finished his thoughts of the past. Even though he missed the times, he would have to leave them there. He was in the present, and that was war. Upon walking into the armory, he adopted a serious demeanor and scanned for Frank. The man wasn't seen in the immediate vicinity, so he decided to walk up to the counter and ring for him.

"One moment," Frank called from somewhere in the back. Seconds later a section of the walls behind the counter sank into the ground, and he walked out of a secret room.

"Are there a lot of those here?" JD asked as he noticed Frank holding what seemed to be a new type of grenade.

"Oh, it's you, Mr. Koffee." His voice seemed neither annoyed or excited. "How may I help you?"

"I was wanting to get a heads up on any details you may have on the next mission. Just wanting to be prepared and all."

"You know that when it comes time, you will be given all the information you need to be given for the appointed mission."

"I know," JD paused. "It's just that I want to be better. The last mission went horribly, and I want to become a better soldier in hopes of preventing things like that in the future. One way I thought I could start is by planning a mission ahead with whatever available mission I have."

Frank stood there for a few moments contemplating JD's words before he spoke again. "Look, Mr. Koffee, you are a fine soldier. You received high marks from the time you joined until now. You just have to mature as a soldier. You've stepped into a pretty big role, and it will beat you down. I'm not promising you won't lose the ones you love or care for, because you will. No matter how far ahead you may plan with whatever information you are given, something will eventually go wrong. This is what I can tell you, though: it's okay. You are only human, and as long as you try your best with the best of intentions, then you are going to be just fine." The wise words hit JD hard, and guilt from his prior actions toward Frank poked at him until he had to say something.

"I'm sorry," he said suddenly.

"For what?"

"First mission briefing. I am a grown man, a soldier, and I acted like a child. I wanted to apologize. I shouldn't have acted like that."

"That's quite fine." Frank laughed a bit. The laughter confused JD. "Although the actions of your team aren't very proper, they define who you are. You're mostly innocent to the horrors of war, and your happy-go-lucky disposition shows that. Want to know what I think?"

"Sir?"

"Have fun while you can. One day you're going to have seen and done enough that there will barely be a glimmer of that innocence left. Reality will have swallowed you. Keep it for as long as you can. Whether you notice it or not, it helps those around you to see a special light. One that keeps them going. Even myself."

"Thank you, sir," JD responded. He was beyond grateful for the words that were given to him. He had never looked at things that way before, and it was a nice change of perspective.

"No, thank you." Frank smiled back. "May I ask a favor of you?"

"Anything." His answer was immediate.

"Would you mind helping me clean weapons today? I have a good amount to do and no help."

"Yes, sir." JD smiled and Frank motioned toward the secret passage. The whole conversation had been a great experience. It had shown him that many others look to people like him, many he wouldn't even guess, for a bit of light to guide them through their day.

JD spent the rest of the day and into the night helping Frank around the armory. Before he went back to the hotel, he made sure to visit Damien and see how he was doing. His condition was the same, but the doctors hinted that there had been some type of activity and that he could wake up as soon as the next day. The news had been a perfect way to end JD's day. He made his way to the hotel and up to the room. When he entered, he saw Peter passed out on his bed, and he couldn't help but smile.

"A lot of the times, you can be our light, bro. Thank you," he said as looked at his sleeping friend. A moment later he lay down and let the thought of Laurielle fill his mind. Soon he was asleep and dreaming, for the first time in a long time.

CHAPTER 6

Peter - A Friend in Need

Night of Incident

Peter was uneasy as he watched Damien lie unconscious on the hospital bed. He had come so close to losing his friend. Had he not grabbed Damien as he was falling from the helicopter, the bed would be an empty one, and Peter would be asking for a transfer back to Earth. He looked over at JD and wondered what he was thinking.

"I really hope he wakes up soon," JD finally said. His chin rested on his hands.

"Me, too," Peter responded, his voice low and his gaze cast on the floor. He thought back to a few weeks before when he had finally received the orders to come to the planet. Excitement had flowed through him, and he was ready to get here and take control. He had felt invincible. Their first mission had added to that, newbies in the field receiving no injuries and high marks, but the last mission had given him a small glimpse of reality. They weren't invincible, and anyone could disappear at any time.

"You think he is going to be okay?" Peter asked his friend.

"Yeah, the doctor said there shouldn't be anything to worry about."

"I didn't mean it like that. I'm talking about Moriah. He seemed to really care about her. Don't really know their past, but they seemed close, and he lost her."

"We'll be there for him to make things better. Plus, I was there moments after she was gone, and I saw some screen. Apparently she is safe somewhere on Saturn."

"Saturn?"

"Look, Pete, this place is crazy, and I don't understand any of it much. I do know that we were sent here to do missions to help end this madness. Maybe we'll find the answers in the meantime. But right now, I just want to relax and have what I can under control. You should do the same." There was a long silence before he got up and left Peter by Damien's bedside.

"Not even a day without you, bud, and we're already not ourselves. Hope we have you back soon." Peter stood up from his chair and turned to see Josiah staring in through a window. His expression was sad, and his cheeks seemed a little red. It was then that Peter remembered that Moriah was his sister, and he went to meet Josiah in the hall.

"Has he been awake to say anything about my sister?" Josiah said as soon as Peter approached. His voice was strained. It had only been hours since he had lost his sister.

"No," Peter replied in a sympathetic tone. "But JD told me what he knew."

"Just tell me she's not dead." His voice choked a bit as the words left his lips.

"Apparently she was transported safely to some type of installation on Saturn."

"What?" Anger was slowly entering his voice. "We know nothing of an installation there, and with as old as this technology is, something could malfunction, and she could die at any moment, and we won't be able to save her, and we'll lose her, too, and I won't know what to do." Josiah was growing frantic, and Peter didn't know what to do, so instincts kicked in. He quickly brought Josiah close for a hug.

"It's okay, buddy," he said quietly as he patted Josiah's back. "We can't change what happened. We can only change where we go from here and how we take what happened." Peter could tell his instincts were right. Josiah's breathing was starting to calm.

"Thanks, Peter," he said while pulling away. "It's just hitting me hard because we lost Mom not too long ago. She was one of the first through the portal. Moriah, Dad, and I were just coming to terms with her disappearance, and now Moriah is gone. I know the risks of this line of work, but that doesn't mean it hurts less."

"You just need to get your mind off all the bad. Just know she is safe right now. How about you hang out with me for a little while? Damien being injured has taken a little toll on JD and me, so I'll need someone to hang out with as well."

"That actually sounds like a good idea, but I can't tonight. I need to report to headquarters before the night is over. Meet you in the lobby of your hotel tomorrow morning?"

"Sounds great, man," Peter said as he looked through the window at Damien.

"Can't change what happened, Pete. Go from here. See you tomorrow." Josiah turned and started to walk away but stopped to turn to Peter. "Thanks again." Peter smiled in return, took one last look at Damien, and started on his way to the hotel.

The sky on base was clear, and the stars shone brightly. It was hard to believe that just earlier in the night, everyone was running for their lives in the pouring rain. Peter walked the side street and wondered what he would do the rest of the night. JD had gone off on his own, and Damien was injured as well as not awake.

"I wish I could learn where the Prisoners came from, how they began," he suddenly said to himself as he walked. "With enough information, maybe I could do something."

Like Damien, Peter had also joined the war to try to change things. He hoped he could be just what was needed. He hadn't always had his sights set on the military, however. Before the military, he had wanted to be a comic book artist, but that soon fell through. He eventually followed his brother into the military, but during his time at boot camp, he found out that a portal had been opened and that his brother had been killed on the planet. Grief had struck him hard, and all he could think of was revenge. Soon, he was put on a team with two people that had become his best friends. They had changed a lot of things for him.

Reflecting on the past had taken up a great deal of time and the hotel was soon in sight. Tiredness from the mission and stress was slowly creeping over him. As he entered the lobby, he scanned hopefully in search of JD but could not find him anywhere. Instead of searching, he went for the elevator and went up to the room. Upon entering, he saw JD already passed out, and Damien's bed was empty. A slight sorrow washed over him, and he lay down in his own bed. He just wanted everything to be okay and back to normal. Wrapping up in blankets, he closed his eyes and then suddenly smiled.

"Everything is going to be alright," JD said.

"I know, bud," he replied. With that, the two of them fell asleep.

Chapter 6.1

Peter - An Object in Motion

1 Night After Incident

Peter's eyes flickered open to the sunlight streaming in through the window, and it seemed to have its warmth, which was something that confused him. The planet appeared to have a moon and stars in the sky, but the sun of the planet was absent. All the light and everything it could produce was there, but the star itself wasn't.

He turned on his side to notice that JD wasn't in his bed. Peter had no idea where he could have gone off to, but he thought that it may have been for the best since he had set aside the day to hang out with Josiah. One thing was first on his list, however: he had to go visit his friend in the hospital. With any luck, Damien would be awake.

It didn't take long for Peter to get ready and make his way down to the lobby. As he stepped out of the elevator, he was surprised to see Josiah sitting on a couch in the lobby, waiting on him. Peter didn't know he had meant this early in the morning. Regardless, he made his way over to his friend.

"Hey, bud," Peter announced as he approached.

"Hey, Pete," Josiah said in a slightly melancholy tone. "What are the plans for the day?"

"Well, first I wanted to go check on Damien. Then we'll just see where we go from there. How's that sound?"

"Sounds good to me. I have a pretty clear schedule until this evening. Then I'll have to go to headquarters for a mission briefing."

"Well, let's get started then!" Peter said happily as he headed out of the lobby with Josiah trailing closely behind him. It wasn't long till Josiah was by his side and talking.

"So what brought you here, Pete?" Josiah asked.

"What do you mean?"

"Why did you come here to fight the Prisoners? I read your team's background before you came here. I know you were close to being a successful artist but something made you change your direction."

"My brother." Peter laughed a little then his face turned stoic. "I looked up to him so much. When we were younger, he loved art but never followed it. So I wanted to use my talent to create things for both him and me. Soon, he entered the military, and I loved that he wanted to fight for freedom and save people. I felt I could do more for humanity by doing that as well. So a while after he went in, I quit art school and decided to join him. I was training when the portal was opened. I got a letter telling me that he had orders to go in and that he would see me soon. That was the last I ever heard from him. A couple of weeks later I received the news that he had been killed in action on this planet. I became so broken and full of rage. I wanted to kill and destroy what had killed my brother and destroyed me. So I asked to be transferred into the new training program meant for soldiers coming here. That's where I met Damien and JD." He paused and laughed a little bit. "Sorry for rambling; just kinda got carried away on my story. Never really told anyone."

"That's fine," Josiah replied as he silently thought to himself. "I like hearing about what brought people here. Tells you a lot about who they are."

"So why are you here?" Peter flipped the question.

"Well, I wish I could say it was as easy as I kept the family tradition going," he laughed, and the comment made Peter smile as well. "But the thing is, I didn't want this at first. I had an office job where I made good money. Easy life and everything. Was trying to break away from the family tradition of giving my life to the military. Soon, however, the company I was working for was shut down, and I had to find something new. I had plenty of money saved up to get me through a year or two of being unemployed, but then my sister came to see me one day. She was the one who inspired me to go against the tradition, but what she came and told me changed my perspective. I remember her saying that she joined the military and was about to head off to camp. Her choice perplexed me, and I had no idea why she had chosen the path she did. Then she told me that it was for the best. That it wasn't about following tradition. It was about giving up your life daily to give others life. To see the smile of the broken and to give hope to the ones you protect. To be a guardian to the helpless."

"I really don't know much about her, but she sounds like a pretty amazing person," Peter said as they finally approached the hospital and he opened the main entrance door for Josiah to walk through.

"Thanks," he said in response to the kind gesture, "and she is an amazing person. I know you can see Damien thinks the same. I just hope when he wakes up that he won't take it too bad. Sure I don't like what he did to her when they were younger, but I'd never wish heartbreak on someone."

"Heartbreak can do more than erode you mentally. It can do physical damage as well. Damien is strong though, and he has us. I'm just glad you're doing fine."

"I am still sad, but I know there is a glimmer of hope in all of this. I just need that glimmer to shine a little brighter, and maybe it will in time."

The two of them were quiet all the way up to Damien's room. Upon reaching the window that looked into the room, Peter saw a doctor standing over his sleeping friend. Peter motioned to the doctor in a way that asked if Damien had woken up yet. The man shook his head with slight sorrow on his face.

"Keep positive, Pete." Josiah patted him on the back. "It's only been a day. He could wake up within the next hour for all we know." Peter's face suddenly started to contort in confusion as he saw the doctor hooking something up to Damien.

"What is that?" he said as he leaned forward for a better look. Josiah glanced at the object as well.

"Looks like just another medical tool."

"It's glowing white and pulsing. I've never seen anything like that before."

"I'm sure everything is fine, Pete. Probably just some new monitoring system. More than just your weapons have been improved from the discovered technology of this planet."

"True, I didn't think of that. Hopefully it makes him better."

"They're trying all they can. Let's talk about something different. What did you think of your first mission?" Peter found it to be a bit of an odd subject change but went with it.

"I think it went over well. Not sure how I felt about killing all the Prisoners, though." Josiah laughed in response.

"Why? They're just killing machines. They see you, they kill you. Nothing like their former selves."

There was silence, and Peter slowly looked to him, confusion written all over his face. "'Nothing like their former selves?' I thought that was only a theory." The look on Josiah's face showed that he had messed up.

"Look, can I trust you with something?"

"Of course."

"One of the first Prisoners that was killed had a DNA analysis performed on it. It had small pieces of DNA matching some of our own. We think a long time ago they may have been something like us until something happened. Currently, we have no idea what that something was."

Peter didn't know what to think of the new information he had been given. He stood in silence for many moments as he shifted his gaze to Damien. The doctor had left the room, and he lay motionless. Peter watched his chest to make sure he was breathing. The monitors had shown he was, but seeing the rise and fall of his breaths brought Peter relief. He then focused back on Josiah.

"Are we doing anything with this information?" Peter asked inquisitively.

"How do you mean?"

"We know they used to be like us at one point in time. Does their brain function still resemble ours? Is there any hope of reason within them?"

"I honestly don't know. All I know is the little bit I can get out of my dad. My rank doesn't warrant much information and neither does yours. We're both pawns."

"Even a pawn can make it to the other side of the board and become the strongest piece. Never underestimate a pawn."

"You know," Josiah grinned, "you have a point. I really like your positivity. Look, Damien is still sleeping, so how about we go ahead and go have some fun today? Neither of us has mission duties to attend right now."

"Sounds like a plan. What do you have in mind?"

"Arcade and whatever else we can think of. Just some well-deserved downtime."

"Let's go!"

The rest of the day was spent bonding and getting closer as friends. Peter started to see Josiah as a brother, just like he viewed Damien and JD. Their day only wound down when darkness had set in outside.

"Thanks, Pete," Josiah said as he gave his friend, his brother, a hug. "You're the only one really keeping me out of a dark place right now."

"No one deserves to be left in the dark, having to crawl out alone."

"You're great, bro. Oh, Dad said he wants to see you tomorrow. He said he'll be at his office all day, so it doesn't matter when you show up, but try to keep it in the afternoon if you can."

"That'll be no problem. Do you know what he wants?"

"Not at all. I need to go, though. Pretty tired and still have the walk back to my place."

"Alright, have a good night."

"You as well."

After Josiah walked out of the hotel, Peter made his way up to his bed. As he exited the elevator, he saw JD just reaching the door to the room. Peter wondered where he had been all day, but he wouldn't ask. He knew something had been off with JD since Damien's accident, and even though he had reassured Peter that everything was okay, Peter wasn't going to push it.

"Hey, Pete!" JD called out with an enormous smile. The grin caught Peter off guard, and he instantly started to question in his mind why JD was so happy all of a sudden.

"Hey, bud," he replied with a smile of his own as he approached. "You're pretty happy, huh?"

"Oh yeah! You can add a tally to my name!" It all clicked in an instant. JD had met a girl, and she had said yes to him.

"No way! That's great, man!" Peter embraced his friend and let go. "What is she like?"

"You actually met her once. Actually, you tallied her as a rejection."

"Really? What changed her mind?"

"No idea, and I really don't care. I have a date when we get back from our next mission, and it's the first in a long time. I can't wait to tell Damien!" The words caused a silence that Peter broke with a voice that then had considerably less emotion.

"Did you go see him today?"

"I did. He was still sleeping, and the doctors still have no idea when he will wake up. They were using some strange equipment I have never seen before, so hopefully that stuff will do the trick."

"Yeah, Josiah was telling me about that. He said the equipment they are using is derived from the technology they've discovered here."

"Oh," he said with a pause. "How is he? Is he still mad at me?"

"He's doing good. Actually hung out with him all day. He really needed it. I don't think he's mad at you anymore. He's over the initial shock and thinking clearly now. Are you mad at him?"

"No, honestly, I would have done the same if I was put in his situation. I should have kept a closer eye on her, though. He is right about that."

"Well, we can't change what happened, so let's just go from here."

"From here I want to get out of the hallway and into bed. I'm exhausted."

"Same!"

The two entered the room and got ready for the night's sleep. Both were happy that they were back to normal again. The only other thing they wanted was to have Damien with them, and they knew that would come in time. As sleep covered them both, they smiled contently.

Chapter 6.2

Peter - The Assignment

2 Nights After Incident

The night had treated Peter well. He had woken up rested and happy. When he awoke, he saw that JD was once again gone.

"Am I always the last one to wake up?" he sighed.

It didn't take him long to get ready for the day, and when he finished, he remembered that he was supposed to go see Avery. Curiosity crept inside and caused a little excitement to flow within as well.

He made his way out of the hotel and into the bright light of the ongoing day. After a while of walking, he stopped immediately and froze. A long sighing breath escaped him, and he hung his head.

"Where is Avery's office?" he questioned himself. He had gotten so worked up and in a good mood that he started his day without a plan.

"I'll go ahead and go check on Damien and find a map while I'm there."

As he walked to the hospital, he wondered what Avery wanted with him. He wondered if he was possibly getting a promotion or even a message from home. The thought of a message from his family made him smile even bigger. All the thoughts of the possibilities ran through his mind as he made his way to the hospital and to Damien's room.

His thoughts went quiet as he sat beside his motionless friend. After a moment, he started to speak to Damien of all that had happened to him the past few days. He made sure not to leave out that JD had met a girl.

"And don't worry about Moriah. I know your heart is hurting, but we're going to fix everything. No matter what it takes. I promise." Peter looked for a reaction on Damien's face, but not even the smallest of smiles was seen. Peter got up and walked away. He had to leave while he was still positive.

He found a map of the installation on the front desk of the hospital and began scanning it for the major's office. It didn't take him long to find it, as it was close to the building that actually held the portal. Finally knowing his destination, he started off and let his mind flow once more with the possibilities of the conversation he would be having soon.

It had only taken him ten minutes to walk from the hospital to the office. Once inside, he went to the front desk and told them the reason for his visit. The lady who occupied the desk asked him to take a seat as she contacted Avery.

Moments after he had taken a seat, Avery appeared and called for him to follow. Peter wasted no time in getting up and moving forward. He walked through a door that Avery held open and into the office. Peter looked around and noticed family photos, shelved achievements, and souvenirs spread around the office. It seemed like just another office until he looked into the far corner. He couldn't believe what he was seeing.

"Sir, I'm taking that one day, sorry in advance," Peter said as he stared at it.

"No, you are not, Marin," Avery said in such a serious voice that Peter even wondered why he made the comment in the first place. However, he knew one day he would have to at least try to steal it as a prank. "That is the first Screamer I ever killed. I had it stuffed. Mine. Not yours."

"Yes, sir," Peter said with a smile from his inner thoughts.

"Now take a seat, please," Avery said as he took his own. Peter did as he was told and waited for Avery to begin the conversation. Instead, he sat there in silence as Avery went through papers, the content of which Peter had no idea.

"Sir?"

"Yes?" He looked up and then back to the papers.

"Did you just want company?"

"Yes. Now be good company and be quiet."

"Are you seriou—"

"Shhh, good company." Peter's eyes widened. Of all the possibilities he had considered for what he was called for, being quiet company was not one of them. As the moments passed, Peter was more and more blown away by it all until Avery finally spoke again.

"I'm just kidding. I really did ask you to come here for a reason. How was your first mission?" The question was a familiar one, and he answered it the same way he had to Josiah.

"And what about the second mission?"

"Well, I'll admit, I felt invincible from the success of the first mission, but I quickly learned that is not how it is. The second mission was a reality check for me."

"I've heard that you've mentioned interest in the Prisoners a number of times. A positive interest. Why is that? They killed your brother without a second thought."

"I have seen and been taught about them. They communicate with each other, they strategize, and much more. I feel that creatures with that high of an intelligence level can be reasoned with if done correctly."

"Have you ever tried reasoning with a pack of wolves? They do all of what you mentioned. You don't see us reasoning with wolves and telling them not to kill certain things or even fight with us."

"Sir, I believe they are even more advanced than wolves. They are capable of a lot."

"So what do you expect us to do? Tell soldiers that there is a chance to communicate with them. I don't want anyone to try and think they can be the ones to communicate and do it in the field. It can end in their death and that of many others. We can't show these creatures any mercy. They are mindless killing machines."

"I just think that can change."

"You're not going to give up on this idea are you?"

"No, I believe that if they can be changed, neither side has to die anymore."

For what seemed like a long amount of time, Peter watched Avery contemplate something. He wondered what it could even be, but his answer was only moments away.

"Peter, what I'm about to show you is top secret. If I even suspect you of telling anyone, including your team, you will be kicked out of the military without hesitation." His tone was cold, hard like a blade at Peter's throat.

"I won't tell a soul, sir," Peter faintly said.

"I'm serious, Marin." Avery's stare was unwavering. Peter could feel the gravity of the situation. He knew that whatever he was about to learn was something only very few knew.

"Yes, sir." His voice was more confident now.

"Then follow me." Avery got up from his chair and walked out of the office with Peter close behind him. They made many turns within the building and eventually came to an elevator. It had many security protocols including fingerprint, retina, and body scanning. After all the requirements had been met, the doors opened, and the two stepped in as the doors shut.

Peter felt his gut rise and fall many times as they descended deeper and deeper underground. Avery kept his silence, and Peter decided it would be best for him to do the same. It wasn't long before the doors opened and revealed their destination. He immediately was in awe.

"Welcome to the labs," Avery said with a grin on his face.

"What exactly is this place?" Peter asked as he looked over all the mesmerizing technology, each more incredible than the last. Scientists were walking everywhere and held many strange objects.

"This is where your weapons were produced. There are still things I'll have to keep classified from you, but I can tell you what the purpose of this facility is. This planet is riddled with amazing technology. Some we wouldn't even theorize about in the next fifty years. So, we've been taking what we find, bringing the artifacts here, and reverse engineering them."

"I really don't know what to say," Peter said as they walked past a group of scientist testing what seemed to be a new grenade. It had a few targets around it. One scientist hit an activation button and walked away. Seconds later it levitated into the air and sent out a spherical, white pulse within a short radius and stopped. Anything within that radius turned into white, glowing particles. A split second later, the frozen radial blast disappeared, and all the white particles of the targets turned back to normal. What happened next made Peter grin in awe. Those same particles fell to the ground like a fine sand, leaving the targets with a large and smooth, curved cut.

"We plan on having those field tested within a few weeks," Avery said as he looked in on the scientists cleaning up the mess.

"So what am I here for?" Peter said without looking away from the perfect destruction.

"This." He grabbed Peter by the shoulder and turned him to the side. His mouth dropped. He couldn't believe what he was seeing. Fear overwhelmed him, but after a few moments, it was replaced by calmness filled with curiosity.

"I don't understand," he almost stuttered. He still couldn't bring himself to move. Then Avery stood in front of him.

"Here is the research I want you to study. Learn all of it. Now leave." The voice Avery spoke with was beyond serious. Peter managed to move toward the elevator, but his mind couldn't. It was still back where he was petrified. He was still trying to figure out exactly what he had seen. As he entered the elevator, he heard Avery call to him.

"Not a word, Peter. I mean it."

"Yes, sir," he said as the doors shut on his stunned face. He was still trying to process all he had just witnessed.

Everything was on his mind all the way to his hotel room. He was numb with information, and he knew he couldn't spill any of it. It was when he sat on his bed with the folder of paper in front of him that he let his excitement seep. A wide smile slowly spread, and a joyful but small laugh escaped from him. He spent the rest of the day going over the information he had been given, and his curiosity grew with every read sentence. Hours passed but only felt like minutes to him. It wasn't long till he had to call his day over. JD still wasn't back in the room, but he figured that he was out having fun with his new friend. Sleep held Peter tightly, and he was content.

CHAPTER 7

First of Nightmare

D amien's eyes slowly opened, and a bright light filled his vision. Something soft could be felt under him. There was a constant beeping sound, and he could hear conversation faintly. After a few seconds, after he regained focus, he realized that he was in a hospital room. He reached for his head and found that it was tightly wrapped in cloth. His memory was blurred. He remembered escaping from the nest, but he had awoken in a hospital. Suddenly, a door opened, and his teammates walked in. They appeared to be fine, which made him sigh with relief. Both sat down in chairs next to his bed, and JD leaned toward him. Damien thought he was about to whisper something to him, but he was smacked in the face instead.

"Ow! What the hell!"

"That's for not wearing your seatbelt when we were taking off."

"Yeah," Peter added, "that wasn't very smart."

JD had a smile on his face, and Damien knew that JD was just glad that his friend was all right.

"The doctor said that you'll have to stay one more night," Peter said. "You had a pretty bad concussion. You almost fell out of the helicopter, but I grabbed you."

"Thanks, Pete. How long was I out?"

"Roughly three days. You were knocked out. We got back the same day, and you were rushed straight here. Two full days have passed since then. Doctor said it was a temporary coma. All is fine now. While you were out, JD and I tried to get a Screamer as a pet. Finally got him to go along with it. It was shot by military officers when we brought it to the hospital to check for rabies and all that."

"Did you really bring one on base? Let alone to a hospital?" Damien's eyes were wide with concern as he looked between the two.

"No," JD replied. "We didn't even go try and find one. It's become a little more dangerous out there than usual. We'd probably need a full squad to safely catch just one Screamer."

"Maybe in time we'll get one," Peter added.

"Well, we would like to stay and chat"—JD clapped his hands on his knees as he and Peter got up from their seats—"but we have no missions until you recover. We're going to party at the hotel like usual. See you when you get out."

He and Peter left the room. Damien was alone with his thoughts, and soon all the events that had happened before he was rendered unconscious came to mind. His heart ached as he remembered Moriah vanishing right in front of him. She had come to save him, and he couldn't even do the same for her. He remembered the fear in her eyes before she was taken away from him. It had felt like he was given a second chance when he first ran into her on the base, but then it was gone. As he thought of her, Avery and Josiah walked in.

"I heard the mission was a partial success," Avery said with a sad tone in his voice. Damien knew it was there due to the disappearance of his daughter. "One of your teammates informed me about you knowing the location of the key. Is that true?"

"Do you call losing someone a success at all?" Damien said, glaring at Avery. "Your own daughter."

"Certainly not, but it can't be helped at the moment." Avery's voice seemed to waver. "You know I love my daughter, Damien. I would give anything to have her back here and safe right now." Tears seemed to well up in the man's eyes but would not break down his cheeks. "But I have to focus on the safety of everyone here and possibly the safety of the world.

We can't allow these things to get to Earth." Josiah hadn't spoken a word since entering and seemed to stare off into space. "In any case, I need you to tell me what you learned on the mission. Lieutenant Koffee informed me that you were taken hostage and found later on. What all happened?"

With a sigh, Damien decided to tell him all that had happened.

"I went to clear a room, and upon entering, I was knocked out. When I first came to, I saw a cloaked figure. It began talking to me in perfect English. He showed me a screen with many towers. I could read and understand everything he was showing me. He said he has been watching us and gathering information. Feeding it into the planet's computer or something."

Avery raised an eyebrow. "And what about the towers and the key?"

"Apparently the towers hold something called Nightmare Prisoners, and he pressed a button that released twenty-five of the towers. On the screen, I saw a tower that was on the opposite side of the planet from us. It had a key symbol over it, so I suspect that is where the key is."

Avery was greatly surprised by the news. He immediately stood up and glanced at Josiah.

"It's as we suspected. He is making his move. Inform Damien on his next mission, Josiah. Then come to my office." He swiftly left the room, with Damien looking confused as he left.

"What did he mean by that?" Damien asked. Josiah turned to looked at him and started to speak.

"With the information you have provided, it is clear what your next mission will be. We are to retrieve the key and use it to close the portal. Unfortunately, there is no available aircraft or vehicle to get us there. Prisoners have recently increased in number, and we need all of our crafts. We will have to send your team in a special way. When you're fully recovered, come to headquarters. We'll finish discussing everything there." After saying that, he began to leave but then stopped at the door. "Look, I know what happened to my sister has to be taking a toll on you. Regardless of what happened between you two in the past, I know you really care now and that she really cares for you. Please find a way to bring her home."

"Of course," Damien replied. Sorrow replaced the confusion and filled him, but he held back the tears.

"Thank you. Now I'm gonna go chill with Peter while I can. He's become a good friend the last couple of days. Kinda helped me look for the positive even with my sister being gone. It's just hard with her being gone right after our mother."

"What do you mean?" Damien didn't remember anything about their mother's disappearance being mentioned.

"Moriah never told you?" Josiah's face seemed confused.

"Told me what?"

"Our mother was a scientist here during the first few months of the portal being opened. She was out on a research mission when her team was attacked. Dad said they never found her body, but everyone else on the team was found dead." His voice choked up a bit before he caught himself. "We just don't want to lose Moriah, too."

The words seemed familiar to Damien, and then he remembered the conversation between him and Moriah when they sat upon the roof of the tower. She had talked about not wanting to lose him, too. He didn't know she had lost her mother.

"I'm so sorry. I didn't know."

"It's okay. Get better soon, and go rescue my sister." Josiah gave a smile and shut the door as he left.

For hours, Damien sat in his bed listening to monitors beep. Eventually his doctor came in and took off his bandages. He told Damien that if he really wanted, he could leave at any time but it was advised he stay and rest one more night. The doctor soon left, and he was alone once more. Hours passed, and it became dark outside. He looked around the room and saw three dog tags on a table to his left. One was his, one was Moriah's, and the other was the one he found on his first mission. He reached over and picked it up and found that the markings still looked like it said "Sarah." He wondered about whose it was. If only he had a last name to go with it. It would have to remain a mystery for the time being. He placed the mystery tags on the table, scooping up Moriah's tags and holding them gingerly. He brushed his fingers over her engraved name.

"I never got to make up for breaking your heart, but you still treated me like I had never done anything wrong. You acted like we had never broken up. You even said you loved me." A tear slipped down his cheek as he slipped the chains of both his and Moriah's tags around his neck. He put the mystery tags he had found in his pocket and got ready to leave. The last thing he wanted was to be laid up in a bed.

He made his way down to the lobby and checked himself out. As he walked out of the building, he looked to the sky and wondered about her. He recollected that the computer had said she was on Saturn. It probably knew the name of the planet due to cross-referencing data previously stored on the planet with the data the cloaked figure was giving it. He then remembered that the screen had said she was safe. It was better than nothing, even if he didn't know if he could trust it or not.

Suddenly, there was a loud boom followed by gunshots. Damien froze when a roar erupted from the gunshots. His mind then shot to the thought of the Nightmare Prisoners. Immediately, he questioned whether or not it could be one. One thing he knew was that he was in no way prepared to fight a monster. He hoped the troops could handle it.

The chaos grew closer and closer. Soon a few soldiers came running in from behind him.

"What's going on?" he yelled to one of the troops.

"Captain Rivers, sir," one stopped to answer, "we have a breach, and all troops are being called to take out the target. It isn't much, but take this!" He handed Damien a standard pistol and ran off toward the chaos. Damien looked down at the weapon.

"How can I take out a large Prisoner with this?" he asked himself as he looked up to watch the soldier run off. Then his heart beat hard. The monster burst through a building and immediately began its assault on the soldiers. Shot after shot was fired, and soldier after soldier was quickly taken out. Damien stood frozen in place. He didn't know how he could stand a chance. The monster was gigantic and had a completely armored body. His small firearm wouldn't do a thing. The feeling of being useless killed him. Then the monster jerked its head toward him.

"Please don't see me," he said to himself. "Please don't. Please." It stepped toward him and unleashed a frightful roar. "Crap." The monster broke cement as it began its charge toward him but was stopped short by a bus plowing into its flank from a side street. The creature stumbled over and slammed into a building, collapsing as the bus backed up and made its way to Damien as he stood there stunned. So much had just happened in less than a minute.

As the bus pulled up, the doors opened, and he saw Peter in the driver's seat.

"Get in!" he yelled. Damien looked at the Prisoner and saw it was getting up from its fall. It looked at him and released a deafening roar. He wasted no time getting on the bus. Once on, Peter slammed on the gas pedal, and the machine lurched forward. "Go help JD!"

Damien looked to see that JD had the back door open, with a wide variety of weapons placed in the seats next to him. He had his rifle and was unloading rounds on the beast. Round after round was deflected, and the creature began its assault forward, giving chase.

"How do we take it out?" Damien asked as he approached JD.

"I have no idea. We were in the armory when we heard it bust through the gate. So naturally we took what we needed and commandeered a bus. I just now started trying weapons on it." Damien watched as cement broke from the strides the Prisoner was making.

"No identifiable weak points?"

"All I can see are the slots its eyes see out of and whenever it opens its mouth. Can't hit the ey—" He was interrupted as Peter flung the bus around a corner and onto the next street, knocking over a light pole. "Can't hit the eyes because it won't stop moving. If we time it right, we can shoot its mouth when it roars."

Damien looked at the monster and realized it was dangerously close. It swung its massive arms and razor-sharp claws at the bus. JD ducked along with Damien as the top back of the bus was taken off. Sparks flew in the air, and then the opening presented itself. The monster's mouth was agape and attempting to go in for a bite. That's when Damien pulled out the pistol and unloaded several rounds into the roof of its mouth. The Prisoner reeled back, shaking its head.

"Did that kill it?" JD asked as Peter brought the bus to a stop.

"Why'd you stop, Pete?" Damien yelled.

"Tanks," he called back. Once he answered, Damien looked toward the front of the bus and saw a line of tanks up the street. Each had its sights trained on the creature. Suddenly, one of the men from the line called out.

"Get out of the bus and run this way. We are about to open fire." Damien looked to JD, and both started sprinting at once. In seconds, they had reached the front of the bus and exited along with Peter. Damien looked over his shoulder and saw the Prisoner had regained its composure and was running at them once more. Then it was over. All the tanks began firing over the team's heads and impacting the monster. Pieces of armor were blown off, and finally, a round found its way through. An arm was blasted away, and the creature collapsed to the ground. Its blood was like acid and dissolved away the cement as it pulled itself closer with one arm. The barrage of explosions did not cease until the Prisoner did so as well.

Damien and his team stood behind the line of tanks with covered ears. They stared at the dead monster that lay just in front of where the bus had stopped. The thing had survived many rounds from the tanks before it was brought down. If Damien had not shot inside its mouth, then he and his team might not have bought enough time to get to safety.

"Area secure," a soldier nearby said. He then walked over to Damien and his team. "How are you?"

"We're fine. Luckily."

"Good. We'll take it from here. We've increased security on base and tightened defenses. Nothing else is getting in here tonight. I suggest you all go get rest. I have the feeling a lot is going to be happening in the coming days, and we're going to need everyone we have."

"Good idea," Damien replied as he turned to walk in the direction of their apartment, followed by his team. It didn't take them long to reach their room and lie down. All of them were really tired and just wanted to sleep. Damien again thought about Moriah, and as he fell asleep, a tear fell down his cheek. He missed her.

CHAPTER 8

Departure

The entire night had been full of restless sleep for Damien. He had woken up countless times from the nightmares that plagued him. They had been Moriah vanishing before him, with nothing he could do. Soon, he could sleep no more and decided to stay awake. It wouldn't be long before he would have to get up. He looked over and saw JD spread out on his bed. A moment later, after looking around more, he saw Peter passed out on the balcony.

"Not sure I wanna know," Damien said to himself as he sat on the edge of his bed.

The minutes flew by as he lay there and let overwhelming thoughts fill his mind. He wondered what he could have done that night to have saved her. Then the Alpha flashed inside his mind.

"Was she a part of his plan?" he asked himself. He knew the Alpha had large amounts of information on everyone and everything. It still didn't explain how he would have known Moriah would be the first to find him. Perhaps it was just by chance. The thoughts were like a savage hurricane in his mind and lasted until the first light of day when the phone started to ring.

He didn't have to answer it to know what it was about. It would be regarding his team's next mission and a given time to report. Even though he knew all it would consist of, he knew he had to answer.

"Hello?" he said as he kept his voice down. He didn't want to wake JD and Peter, and the previous ringing had not.

"Damien, it's Avery," the man said. "How are you doing?" It came as a bit of a surprise to Damien that Avery would ask him such, let alone lead with it.

"Yes, sir," he said in a bit of a monotone. "Night was a little rough but I'm fine. How about yourself?" He felt as though Avery was needing someone to show they cared. It was out of character for him to ask Damien how he felt, and he knew the man was hurting after losing his daughter.

"My nights may never get better," he said. His voice seemed distant as though he was off in thought as he spoke. "Only time will tell. When this is all over, I would like to get to know you. Even if she never comes home. That's what she would want."

"I promise you I will bring her home," Damien said, his voice gaining emotion and strength. "Even if it kills me, I will make sure she is home safe with her family. With us."

"Thank you." He took a quick pause then began business. "Now, I need you and your team to get ready and meet up at the armory. We're putting the final plans into effect. Be there as soon as possible, please."

"Yes, sir," he said, and a moment later he heard the line cut. His heart was beating slow but hard. He knew Moriah's father was trusting that he would find some way to bring her home. That was all he wanted as well.

He turned away from the phone and turned to face his teammates as they lay sleeping. Fear was lurking deep inside of him. The next mission could mean certain death to any of them, and he would be leading them right into it. He had to make sure he would be the best leader he could be and protect them while accomplishing the mission.

It took a few minutes before he decided to wake his team. Surprisingly, it didn't take much effort to do so. They were both up and ready at an astonishing pace. Damien smiled but then let it slowly fall into a frown. They were changing. It hadn't been a week since their arrival, and already so much had happened to change them from who they were before. He just hoped they would never lose themselves and would stay the friends they came as. It was then, while the two finished getting ready, that he witnessed his bit of hope.

"Whoo!" Peter exclaimed as he let out a stretch. "Mission day!"

"Let's own it!" JD chimed in, and then they both turned to Damien, who stood silent. He couldn't help but smile, and his eyes watered. They were his lighthouse in a sea that was only getting more dark and stormy.

"Let's be the difference!" he announced.

It didn't take long before they were out and heading to the armory. Damien had felt sadness as he had walked through the lobby. All he wished was that Moriah would run up to him and that everything would be okay. Instead of letting the sadness overwhelm him, he looked to his teammates for positivity, and they were everything but short. They made him happy in no time.

After their walk to the armory, Peter and JD up to their normal antics along the way, they arrived. Damien walked in the front door and found out that they were the last to arrive. All the other teams for the mission were gathered in the center of the armory. They all were standing in a large circle around Avery and Frank. Avery noticed Damien and gave a small smile then motioned for them to proceed.

"Nice of you to join us," he said as Damien and his team approached. Damien nodded as he stood strong and tall with his team. "Now we can begin the briefing. Frank." Avery stepped out of the way and let Frank have center stage.

"Right, so I know you all know the last mission to a Prisoner nest was far from successful. Due to the MIA and the shortage of time, we weren't able to recover much from the systems. However, what we did recover was enough. The key to the portal lies on the opposite side of this planet, but we can't fly you there."

"Why is that, sir?" a soldier said from the crowd.

"Prisoners have begun making a big move. Far out scouts have reported back and show that large amounts of Prisoner activity are starting to center in on us. From all sides. We can't spare another craft due to the fact that we need all the defense we can get to keep the portal safe. So the alternative? Underground. We have found a large, global rail system. It leads straight to the city that holds the key. If what we have found is correct, we can go to any station and have a transport called to us. You will then take that all the way. We expect you to arrive there within fifteen to twenty-four hours depending on the number of complications. As for evac, we are currently finishing up transport jets. They won't be ready for another day.

We assume you will attract a lot of attention once you get there. A certain target is expected to appear. We will pick you up at the highest point after you have received the key and bring you home. On your way out, we will nuke the city with said target inside with a few high-speed aircraft that are here just for this operation. Any questions?"

"What happens if there is an obscene amount of complications and we don't follow the timeline correctly?" Peter asked. "Is there a chance of us entering the city late and being nuked while inside?"

"Good question. No, you will not be nuked. You will all have long-range communication gear that works off the signals this planet itself gives off. We will know your location and situation at all times. Once everything is clear and safe, the nuke will be waiting locally to be deployed. You will be extracted, and the city will be no more, along with our target." Peter had no objections and waited for more on the mission to be said. Avery took the lead and began to speak.

"All of you here are from the previous mission and will be proceeding with this mission. Now your point of entry will be where SF5-3 had their first mission, where we recovered the belongings of Dr. Wright. You will start the march there and go underground to find a terminal to call for transport. As you wait, set up defenses until it arrives. You will have two scientists accompanying you that will operate the transport to the best of their ability. Josiah will be leading this mission. We will, however, fly you there and provide aerial cover fire until you tell us you have departed. Grab your weapons and gear. You leave now. Meet at the airfield."

Damien's heart was racing, and he thought back to his first mission. As he thought, he pulled the odd dog tags out of his pocket and looked at them. He remembered the dark pathway that was where he found them and knew that was their destination. The thought then occurred that he may find out where the tags had come from. He tossed the thought aside as he felt the cold metal of Moriah and his own dog tags hanging around his neck. For a moment, he reached his hand to them and clenched them tight through his gear. A second later, he let go and turned to his team.

"Let's go."

Each team was heavily armored and geared for battle. It hadn't taken long for them all to suit up and meet at the airfield.

"Strap in this time," JD teased Damien as they walked to their helicopter and boarded.

"Will do," he laughed as he rubbed the spot on his head that he hit the time before. It was a little sore to the touch but seemed to be almost perfectly healed. It was also a reminder that he could not act carelessly.

"I'd still catch you if it happened again, but let's not," Peter joined in.

"How about when we get home we party?" JD asked the two. "By home, I mean Earth."

"I'm not partying until she is home," Damien said seriously. "If I can use any part of this mission to find out how to do it, then I will." His friends were silent as they saw his mood change. He was no longer happy, but determined, and they didn't know how to feel about it.

The flight to the drop zone was quick, and they were dropped on top of the building. Not a single Prisoner had been in sight. Damien saw it as suspicious seeing as there had been reports of large numbers growing closer. Even the inside of the main room in which they had found Dr. Wright had been empty.

Damien walked straight to the dark path and waited for everyone else to form up on him. He dared not look behind, or his heart would hurt. The smell alone made him sad, but it was reality. The picture and the date flashed in his mind, and he fought hard to hold off the tears.

"Lights on!" Josiah said from behind Damien. He could be heard on the headset by all. "Rivers, your team moves forward. Be cautious."

Damien brought his weapon and moved forward with his team close behind. Each checked his corners as he moved forward. He was just glad he was able to leave the surface and proceed. Each step he took was a quiet one and seemed painfully slow. Looking around, he saw the age of the surrounding walls. Roots had sprung out from cracks, and vegetation had partially covered the path. The further down they went, the newer it seemed. Old cement turned into a glistening metal that only bore dust from the ages. Suddenly, the fear on Moriah's faced raced in his mind. He couldn't control his worry for her.

"Damien," he heard JD call. "You're moving too fast. Slow it down a bit." Damien realized that he had been speeding up as he thought of her. He felt a beating in his chest, and all he wanted was to get to the transport.

It took only a couple more minutes for them to reach a large open area that Damien could only assume was the transport launch station.

"Destination reached, sir," he announced over his mic to Josiah in a whisper. The station was gigantic. His light barely reached the top, and as he swung it to the sides, he saw multiple tunnels. Pillars from structural support were scattered about as well. Still, not a hostile was in sight.

"Good. Keep guard on where we came from in case there are other entrances into that pathway that the enemy can take. Team SF2-7, I need you to take one scientist and scout the immediate area for the terminal and call a transport. The rest need to secure this area while we wait." Damien swung his light around and saw that there was the transport system not too far in front of him. It was just an indentation in the ground, with a single rail in the center that stretched and split into the different tunnels.

The teams all went about their orders, and Damien went back to the entrance that led upward. He knelt to the ground and aimed up the pathway while his team stood on each side of him. Finger resting above the trigger, he waited for something to move in the darkness.

"JD, you keep an eye on our three o'clock. Peter, nine o'clock."

"Copy," they both replied in unison.

As they waited, they could hear chatter over the headsets. The scouting team seemed to have discovered the terminal and were figuring out how to operate it.

It only took a matter of minutes before lights came on inside all of the walls. The instant flood of light was a shock, but Damien kept his breathing easy. Then his grip tightened on his weapon. There was a hostile in the pathway that had been just as startled by the sudden illumination. It was a Slasher that was slowly making its way down the pathway toward the teams.

"Sir, we have a lone hostile heading down the pathway. Slasher. It has yet to notice our location. Eyesight must be shot. Orders?"

"We have a few minutes until a transport arrives. Take it out and form up on the other teams."

"Yes, sir," Damien whispered. He put the crosshairs on his target and pulled the trigger. There was a muffled pop and a thud as the bullet made contact with the creature's skull. It crashed to the ground and was motionless. He dropped his weapon and turned around to walk away.

"Hostile eliminated, sir. Proceeding to—" He was cut off by the blood-chilling shriek of a Screamer. He spun to find it had stepped out from a hidden entrance by the Slasher. The monster looked at its downed ally and began sniffing the air. Before Damien could bring his rifle up and fire again, the Screamer jerked its head toward him and ripped a horrible and terrifying noise from its throat. The next second, Damien shot and the creature fell to the ground. The moment it did, however, many other screams started to echo throughout the underground structure. Then came a deep and deathly roar: a Giant Demon.

"Damien!" Josiah shouted over the mic. "Move now! Hostiles inbound. Transport almost here."

He and his team turned around with haste and saw where everyone had gathered near the opposite end of the open area waiting for safety to arrive. As they sprinted for them, they saw a few other teams come out of random doorways and begin their sprint as well.

Finally, Damien caught sight of the transport coming out of a nearby tunnel. A couple tunnels over from it, the Giant Demon burst through with Screamers at its feet. The behemoth grabbed a column and broke off a large chunk, causing the column to collapse. It hurled the massive debris in their direction. The mass of stone and metal slammed into the ground and was skipping around the ground at great speed. Each time it hit the ground, a shockwave went through the soles of Damien's feet. It narrowly missed his team and slammed into another that had been running close beside them. Screams ripped through the air as they were hit, and blood splattered on the ground.

Damien's eyes widened and his paced quickened to the docked transport that the teams were loading hastily into. A few had stayed outside to unleash fire on the incoming creatures. However, they had to fire at a slower rate for more precise shots as to not hit Damien or the other teams. He looked to make sure his team was with him, and they were directly behind.

"Start the transport," he yelled over the mic. His heart was pounding and his breath rushing in and out of him. Suddenly he heard the Giant Demon roar much closer. He spun his head while running and saw the monster barreling toward them on all fours. It crashed through pillar after pillar and was gaining ground.

"Drop a grenade, Pete!" Damien shouted. "Slow it down." Without even responding, Peter pulled out a grenade as he ran, noting the distance of the creature. He pulled the pin and waited a few seconds before he dropped it. They kept running and finally reached the transport that had started moving and was gaining speed. Once they jumped in, Damien looked behind and saw the grenade detonate with fire and fury. The monster's feet were knocked out from beneath it, and it started to tumble. Pillars gave way as the creature plowed into them. It was then that Damien heard a loud crack that was the start of many. The Giant Demon had taken out so many pillars that the structural support was not enough to hold up all that was above.

It started as small stones and chunks of dirt then turned into boulders and mounds of earth. The ceiling collapsed on top of the monster and was taking out all the Screamers and Slashers. Each screeched in horror as one by one they were buried under the rubble. The collapsing building was catching up with their transport.

"Hold on!" Josiah yelled, and Damien and his team made sure to grab onto the nearest hold. The lights inside the transport began to flicker, and the floor shook. Then it was just a distant noise as Damien felt the sheer speed the transport had gained. He looked up and saw that they were in a tunnel and heading onward to their destination. They were safe for the moment.

"Five hours till this thing has to stop and charge. Rest up until then."

Damien took the words and followed them. After making sure his friends were okay, he proceeded to find a spot to rest. Soon, without even realizing it, he had fallen asleep.

CHAPTER 9

A Warning

JD watched as his friends slept. The previous encounter with Prisoners had been a close one, and a few soldiers had even died. He hadn't known them personally, but they were still his brothers in arms, so their loss still hurt him. Relief that he was still alive and well flowed through him but then vanished. His mission, the one he was given specifically, was beginning. He just had to figure out how to get alone when they stopped. He would be putting himself at death's door and hoping it wouldn't answer. A few hours would pass before he had his plan in order.

It wasn't long before Laurielle found her way into his mind. He couldn't wait to get back and see her. There were so many plans he wanted to make. But all of that would have to wait. A sliver of sadness went through him as he looked at Damien. JD was able to make plans while Damien had to hope for a way to save the one he loved. He tried to put himself in Damien's shoes and feel the pain that he was going through. No matter what he thought, he knew he was never going to reach the amount of pain that Damien was feeling, the amount of helplessness. Then guilt washed over him. His friend wouldn't be hurting if he had kept an eye on her. If he had kept her safe, maybe they would all be safe and happy. JD knew that blaming himself was a dangerous thing. It could consume him were he not careful.

"You don't even know it is my fault she's gone do you?" he whispered as he looked at Damien while he slept. "Even if you knew, you still wouldn't blame me. You'd just say that you should have done something different, that you shouldn't have let her do this or that. You would blame yourself for getting captured before you would even blame me. I'll make it up to you, bro. You're not doing this alone."

The entire transport of troops was silent for the duration of the ride. Hours passed before JD could feel a change in momentum. He shifted forward as the transport slowed. His nervousness was starting to rise even more. It would not be long before he would deliberately put himself in danger.

"So what is the plan, Josiah?" he asked.

"We reach the charging station, charge, then leave. The scientists said it shouldn't take long at all. Of course, we'll set up defenses as well."

"Private channel." He waited till Josiah was the only one looking and gave him a visual signal from across the transport on which channel to tune to. It was only moments before JD could hear him again.

"Yes?" he said in a hushed voice.

"When we arrive, I need to go alone for a bit, but I need it to be unnoticed that I'm gone. The other teams won't really notice my absence as long as I can sneak off without being seen to begin with. Damien and Peter, on the other hand, they'll keep an eye on me just to make sure I'm safe and will question or act rashly if they see that I'm gone all of a sudden. This is a mission from Avery that I need to complete." Josiah seemed to take a minute to contemplate all that was said before he began his response.

"We'll leave Damien and Peter asleep along with a few of the other sleeping soldiers. They'll need most of their energy anyway. I know Damien hasn't been doing well. Let the soldiers who are awake know that we'll be letting them sleep."

"Yes, sir," JD said as he prepared to switch back to the open channel. "You know, you're pretty strong. It's admirable."

"I'm breaking just as much as he is if not more. I'm just a little better at hiding it. We have a mission to complete. But thanks." The channel cut to static, and Josiah was gone.

"Here we go," JD said to himself as he mentally prepared himself for what was ahead. He made his way around, letting the other soldiers know to not wake the sleeping and to prepare. Soon, the transport stopped, and the soldiers quietly exited and dispersed into the surrounding area to begin the wait.

JD waited till no eyes were facing him then made his way into the nearest tunnel of darkness. His heart was pounding, and fear gripped him. It wasn't until he had made his way into the darkness that he turned on a light. Upon turning it on, he was relieved to find that he was alone. The eerie silence was even a bit comforting.

"Where are you?" he said as he walked ever deeper into the tunnel. He suddenly stopped, and his heart skipped a beat. Footsteps, large ones, were heard directly behind him. A faint green glow had shown up on the wall to either side of him. A Pulser was standing a few feet behind him.

The darkness felt even darker as he continued to stand still. He didn't know why the creature had not attacked but knew there had to be a reason. Slowly, he turned around, weapon at the ready, and faced his pursuer. The being towered a couple feet above him and looked him dead in the eye. Fear was no longer a word to describe what he was feeling. He couldn't think of any word that could describe it.

Suddenly, the Prisoner nodded its head and raised one glowing organic weapon of an arm, as if ordering him to turn and keep walking. JD hesitated to move, so the creature decided to give him an incentive. It stood taller and walked even closer. Once it was close enough, it growled and nudged him forward. He'd started to turn, but the nudge had been a bit forceful and caused him to trip.

"Such a frail creature," came a voice from the darkness. JD lifted his head and saw the familiar figure he had seen once before, the one that was referred to as the Alpha in his papers. "Stand, human."

JD wasted no time in getting to his feet and trying to stand tall. One wrong move could mean death. Then it occurred to him that even the right move could mean death for him.

"I'm here to talk," JD said with a stern voice.

"Oh, are you? What have you to offer?"

"Allegiance. Top-secret information. I don't agree with my species. I want to join your side." He hoped his words were convincing.

"Such a terrible liar," the Alpha laughed. "Why am I to believe you?"

"I have information that will be beneficial to you."

"Don't bother lying. Your side will need as many loyal soldiers as it can get."

"We're reverse engineering technology from this planet and—"

"And you are making your final moves. You're going to close the portal within the next month. Well, it's a surprise to me that it is within far less time. Your troops are preparing for my assault. I know all of this. I know all that you were briefed on, Koffee." JD was stunned and speechless. He had not expected it to unravel nearly the way it had, and he was out of words. "Tell me; why I shouldn't kill you now?"

The pulsing grids on his robe distracted JD from fear as he thought. There was no good reason he could think of why he shouldn't be killed. Anything he could say would just be random and useless. His death could be seconds away.

"Go back to your transport." The Alpha turned around. "You're not even worth my time or energy. This game of chess, as you humans call it, is nearing its end. I will give you a warning to take back, though. It's futile. I will have my revenge. Tell that to Avery." Within seconds, he and the Pulser had disappeared into the darkness, and JD was left alone. He still couldn't bring himself to move. He wasn't sure what had just happened. His stupor was eventually broken by Josiah speaking over his headset on the private channel.

"The transport is ready. Time to go." JD had taken so long to reply that Josiah had to make sure he was there. "Koffee?"

"Be right there," he replied. His voice was distant and as were his thoughts. Eventually, he made his way back, no longer scared of what may lurk in the darkness. He had just been face to face with death and was let go. There had to be a reason.

As soon as he boarded the transport, they were off once more.

CHAPTER 10

Hope's Glimmer

Damien had woken up with Peter leaned up against him, still sleeping. He looked across from him and saw JD sitting and staring off into space. It seemed like something was on his mind. He wasn't quite sure what it was about, but he knew he wanted to find out.

"Are you okay?" Damien asked as he let out a yawn.

"Yeah," JD said with a start, being pulled from his gaze. His attitude adjusted to a happier one. "How was your nap?"

"Good. How long was I out?"

"Five to six hours."

"You've got to be kidding me!" he exclaimed.

"It's fine. We know you haven't had much sleep for various reasons, so we wanted you to get rested so you could focus." Damien knew he couldn't argue much against it. He hadn't had much sleep, and that, accompanied by certain events, caused his mind to wander when it shouldn't. All he could do was hope that the sleep would allow him to focus more on the mission.

"Yeah, I guess." He didn't seem too happy about it but decided not to fight it.

"Five to six hours!" a sleepy Peter suddenly exclaimed. "What's my excuse? I wanted some action."

"Your excuse is, you're Peter," JD responded with a laugh. "And we haven't had any action since we began the ride." His mind momentarily flashed back to the Alpha and Pulser.

"Are you okay?" Damien asked, noticing the vacant look on his friend's face.

"Yeah, you look like you have something on your mind," Peter added.

"I'm fine," JD said quickly. He couldn't let them know what had happened. "Just a little tired myself. A lot has happened so far."

"Well, we're awake now, so how about you get some sleep," Damien suggested.

"Yeah, sure," he replied as he reclined back in the seat he had been sitting in. Within no time he was asleep.

Damien looked around and saw all the troops that occupied the transport. Many were attentive to the passing, blurry scenery, while others were busy attending to their gear. Hours passed, and they had finished their last recharge station and were on the final stretch to the key. Damien then looked to Josiah, who was leaned up against a wall talking to a scientist. His face didn't seem too pleased at whatever the scientist was telling him. After the man walked away, Damien decided to make his approach.

"Everything alright?" he asked as Josiah took notice of him.

"Not exactly," he responded in a voice of slight annoyance. "I'm going to have to contact base and let them know our schedule is going to be pushed back a while."

"How's that?"

"This track ends soon. Approximately one hundred miles away from the city. The scientist said, from what he could tell from the onboard computers, that something is blocking the tunnel."

"Well, when we get to that point, we'll assess the situation and go from there."

"We have about an hour till we figure that out. Be ready." With that, Josiah walked away but then turned and faced Damien once more. "Look. Who knows what is going to happen in this final stretch. Just be careful. She's going to want you to come home to." He gave a smile, but sadness was apparent deep within. Damien didn't know how to respond to what her brother had said. It was something that had stirred him but also gave him a slight feeling of happiness. Her family had come to accept him. Josiah finally walked away to talk to a few soldiers, and Damien was left to think.

"You're gonna be surprised when you get home," he laughed lightly to himself. He made his way back to his team and made sure they were ready for the next stop.

"Definitely," JD said as he checked his sniper. Peter was beside him cleaning his shotgun and making sure all was in order. The hour passed quickly and in silence. Soon, they could feel themselves slowing down.

"File out," Josiah announced as the transport came to a stop. As Damien and his team stepped out, they saw mounds of rubble in front of them. It was old and overgrown with sunlight streaming in through the top.

"Anyone been lifting weight lately?" Peter asked over the headset.

"Yep, I got this." A lone soldier stepped up and walked toward the rubble. "Lifted some this morning."

"Sit down," Josiah laughed. "We aren't getting through here, and I really don't feel it safe to backtrack. I already called headquarters and let them know we've been delayed and that we'll update as we go."

"I thought they could monitor in real time?" Peter asked his friend.

"That was the case, but there has been a malfunction either with equipment or the planet's signals. Either way, communication is going to be slower, and they can no longer track location. Shouldn't be a problem."

"So where do we go from here?" JD questioned.

"Up. We need to get a sense of where we are and where we need to go next. If we're nearly one hundred miles away, then we'll need to find a way there and ration our food." A roar echoed deep from within the tunnel from which they came. There was no telling how far away the creature that it came from was. "Let's move."

There was a nearby tunnel that exited to the ground above. Damien and his team guarded the rear while a new team led the front. Upon reaching the surface, they came out into a clearing. There had been no foundational building, just the exiting tunnel. He looked around to get a sense of his surroundings. It was then that he heard noises that surprised him.

Birds chirped, and the sounds of a rushing stream could be heard somewhere off in front of them. Wind blew softly through the trees and against his face. Light and heat hit his skin from a nonexistent sun. Long blades of grass waved and bent from the gentle touch of the wind. It was like a type of paradise.

"This planet never ceases to amaze me," Josiah said all of a sudden in the headset.

"I agree to that," Peter acknowledged as he, too, took in his surroundings with a look of awe on his face.

"Alright," Josiah began, "we know the tunnel below us runs all the way to the city. We'll travel in that direction. Should we find another entrance to the transport system, we take it. As for now, we walk."

The group kept in a tight formation and pushed forward into the overgrown forest. Trees towered above their heads, and grass brushed against their knees. Everyone proceeded cautiously, wary of the dangers that may lurk in the tall grass. Soon, Damien's team took lead. Just as he got to the front, something caught his eye. Something was shining through the trees, some type of metallic structure. As they grew closer, he realized he had seen it before. It was one of many that the Alpha had shown him.

"Josiah," Damien said in a hushed voice over his mic as he came to a stop.

"What is it?" His tone was alert.

"Nightmare Prison ahead. Orders?" It took a few minutes for Josiah to contemplate on the actions to take.

"Make it a destination."

"Sir?" Damien seemed confused by the order.

"From the intel you gave us, only so many had been released of protective protocol. If it is smart, then it released ones closer to base. So, if this one is indeed safe in reason, then we can check it and gather intel. Possibly find an exact key location and maybe even some intel on Moriah."

That was all Damien needed to hear. He acknowledged his new orders and pushed forward through the forest. A hope had lit inside of him that he may find out how to save Moriah. He wondered if there was perhaps a way to reverse transport her back to the planet and take her home.

Damien saw that the prison was very close after a while of walking. He could see it slightly above the trees as it towered high. With each step, his hope increased even more. He knew it was dangerous to get his hopes so high, but he couldn't help it. They didn't see any more Prisoners on their way there. When they reached the base of the prison, the group saw that it was covered in lush vegetation. Vines ran up its walls that were slanted with different shades of gray. The architecture reminded Damien of human craftsmanship, something of a modern style that an artist would come up with. The entrance was gigantic, and he knew why. It allowed for Prisoners of any size to be transported in or out. That included Nightmare Prisoners. At least one of them was taken care of, he thought, as he remembered the one that had been taken out by the tanks on base. As the group came closer to the entrance, a roar was faintly heard from inside, seemingly from the top.

"Head in and be on guard," Josiah said over the headset as he motioned to Damien. He, along with JD and Peter, walked past the soldiers and entered with their weapons drawn.

They soon found themselves inside a large chamber where a large, circular cavity led all the way to the top. It went so high that it seemed to fade to blackness. There were also the familiar glowing lines spaced across the floor, leading to a glowing circle in the center. Everyone followed them cautiously. The circle glowed brighter as Damien drew closer to it.

"Access that," Josiah said as he walked up beside him. "The rest of you, I want to make sure this place is completely locked down. We also need to find a high vantage point. If you find this place to be safe, then head up high and look toward our destination. Meet back in fifteen." With those orders, everyone but Damien and his team dispersed.

With JD and Peter close by his side, Damien moved to the glowing circle and stepped on it. A bright light sprang from the floor and formed multiple holograms in front of him. Displays of esoteric symbols were shown. He turned to his teammates. "I have no idea what these symbols mean."

"Language: English. Human detected. Initiation of system startup. Issue command," came a voice from the holograms. The symbols shifted to odd-looking English letters, which resembled the writing on the dog tag Damien had found. His eyes widened as he felt the tags in his pocket.

"Where are these from?" he silently asked himself. He had entertained the thought that they had been from a soldier who may have made them for fun. There was still the possibility that someone did just that but had seen the planet's lettering system before and chose that as a base. His thoughts were soon interrupted.

All the walls in sight erupted with light, washing away all shadows, and revealing an impressive sight. The place was quite advanced and well kept on the inside. He wondered if the structure had some sort of automatic cleansing system. JD and Peter looked around in astonishment. Grid patterns pulsed all the way to the top and would occasionally arc from wall to wall. The top was still dark but had something that struck awe. Stars swirled, and some would break away and fall downward. Before they would hit, they'd disappear. Damien turned his focus to the holograms before him. He had things he needed to ask.

"Where am I?"

The holograms immediately replied, "Prison eighty-three, entrance hall."

"What are these prisons for?" Damien wanted to verify the claims of the Alpha.

"These prisons were designed to hold creatures from an unfruitful experiment: the Prisoners."

He pondered for a moment. The Prisoners had just been called an experiment. If the information being told was held to be true, then the Prisoners were never an advanced race but were created by one.

"Who created the Prisoners?"

"Data has recently been deleted."

Damien suspected that the Alpha was responsible for deleting the data. It may not have wanted him to learn of certain matters. He decided to ask another question.

"Has there been any recent transportation activity on this planet?" He had Moriah in mind as he asked the question. The hope from earlier had never diminished in the slightest.

"Affirmative. A human was transported to a safety installation in the home space—"

"Home space?" he questioned immediately.

"Data deleted."

"Is there a way to reverse the transportation?"

"All teleportation sequences are presently shut down."

Damien was dismayed by the answer but pushed forward. "What is the condition of the human who was transported?"

"The human is in a state of hibernation and is on planet Saturn's installation. Video recording received and transferring."

Moriah flashed on the screen, and her body was suspended in air. She looked as she did the last time he saw her. His heart sank at the display, yet he was relieved to know that she was all right. He was determined to find a way to rescue her. He asked his final question.

"Where is the key located in the main prison?"

"The portal key is located within the tower in the middle of the capital city. It is sealed behind doors that have not been opened for many millennia. The city is over one hundred miles north of our present location."

"Understood," Damien replied. He stepped away from the glowing circle and holograms. As he did, the floating panels of light dissipated, and all of the lights began to turn off.

"Oh, come on!" a soldier said over the headset. "The lights couldn't have stayed on?"

"It's fine," Josiah answered. "I heard everything through Damien's mic. We're done here. Let's head out. We have a long hike to begin."

Damien stood motionless as the installation's light system began to power down. He knew what he had to do. Moriah could not be rescued while they were on the planet. He would have to get to Earth and find a way to Saturn. Even though he did not know how to reach her, he told himself that he would. JD and Peter followed behind as he walked away, disappointed that they didn't get the chance to interact with the computer system. The men returned outside and were soon rejoined by the other soldiers. Josiah had begun strategizing for their next course of action. He stated that they were to travel as far as they could toward the capital city with the remaining daylight and set up camp close to nightfall. They would finish the rest of the journey the following days. As everyone departed from the prison, Damien mentally prepared himself for the dangers that loomed ahead.

CHAPTER 11

Words from the Enemy

Not long after the group left the Nightmare Prison, they heard an explosion when they were miles away. Any possible escaped Prisoner could be massive. Josiah gave the order to quicken the pace, and nobody raised any objections. The events at the prison went through Damien's mind. Moriah didn't seem to be in immediate danger, but he knew that to save her he had to do something other than the mission. He didn't know what that would be at that moment, but a thought came his mind regarding their objective. He wondered if his team could stealthily slip ahead to the capital city while the rest of the squads followed behind killing any Prisoners they passed. This would provide an escape route or safe area to fall back to if anything unexpected were to happen. It would be easier to quietly move around with a three-man squad rather than multiple squads that would create a more conspicuous target. Even though the plan had some cons, he felt that it was a good idea. He had to tell his team about it first.

"I have a plan. Hear me out."

"Sure, let's hear it," Josiah replied.

"I want to take my team on ahead to the capital city. We'll be able to move faster and be less visible. You and your men should follow behind to kill any Prisoners that may remain. This will provide both a distraction and a safe area to fall back to if necessary. Only fight if necessary. We don't know how many Prisoners are around."

The group walked quietly while Josiah thought his plan over. After a few minutes, Josiah approved the plan. He acknowledged that it was risky, but the plan was good overall.

"If everything goes well, we will see you back in our world," Josiah said as the team moved forward. "Just please be safe." He held out his hand. Damien hesitated a split second before taking hold of it. The moment he did, Josiah pulled him close and patted him on the back. "Come home so we can rescue her together."

"Of course," Damien smiled.

"Peter," Josiah moved to his friend, "when we get back we're hanging out. You too, JD." He let go after patting Peter on his back as well and faced JD.

"Do I have to?" JD laughed.

"No," Josiah responded, his face turning sad.

"Don't do that," JD glared at him with arms crossed. "You guys know I'm rarely touchy-feely." The moments passed and he caved. The friends said their farewells and proceeded on their own.

After a few minutes, the group was no longer in sight. The forest was thick with vegetation that grew less dense as they moved on. After an hour or so, there was no vegetation. There were only trees that towered and blocked out the sky. The branches acted as a roof that covered the forest. Damien was on point as they traversed the forest, and JD and Peter covered the flanks and rear. They jogged with their pistols held low in front of them. They were on high alert.

After another hour, they slowed their jog to a walk. Something didn't feel right to Damien. The day's end was fast approaching, but they didn't see a single Prisoner. The whole mission hadn't had nearly as many Prisoners as he thought it should have had. He knew something had to be going on.

"We have another mile to go before we reach the mark for the day," Damien announced. "Once we reach it, we'll make camp and get things ready for tomorrow."

"Sounds good to me," Peter said. "Let's go fishing."

An awkward look came across JD's face. "Fishing?"

"Yeah, fishing. You know, where you have a pole, bait it up, and—"

"I know what fishing is! Why would—never mind. Do as you wish. You might as well try to get another Prisoner as a pet while you're at it. We won't be able to take it around military personnel, though."

"No one has time to do any leisure activity until camp is set up. Once that's complete and a perimeter has been established, we can relax for a little while. We have to be up bright and early tomorrow."

The men soon reached an enormous tree that had a giant hollow at its base. The inside was cleared out and free of any debris.

"That's pretty convenient," JD said.

"Not going to lie," Damien replied. "That is pretty convenient."

Damien was relieved by the sight. They wouldn't have to spend much time setting up camp, and they could begin assigning separate duties. JD was assigned to be a lookout for Prisoners within a quarter-mile radius. Peter was assigned to set up trip wires in a two hundred-foot radius around the camp. Damien set up camp inside the hollow. He decided to do without a fire since that would draw attention to them during the night. After he had finished his duty, he waited for JD and Peter to return. As he waited, he thought about the mission, Moriah, and even his home. He questioned whether would be able to complete the mission or not. If a large number of Nightmare Prisoners were to ambush them, they would not survive. He would not be able to rescue Moriah or return home. All the possibilities of everything that could happen were overwhelming, and each took its punch. However, he stood strong and confident that everything would be fine. Negativity was not a demon he could afford to give in to.

It was dark before his teammates returned. The next thing to do was decide who would perform the first watch. Damien ended up receiving the privilege and began to prepare himself. The men were in dangerous territory. Anything could show up. This was especially the case due to the release of the Nightmare Prisoners. He wouldn't be able to take one of those on alone. If he were to spot one, he'd have to alert his team, and they'd leave immediately.

Damien felt that his watch went by slowly, but it was nearing its end. Before it came to an end, however, he spotted a Screamer jump from one tree to another. He grabbed his pistol and had it at the ready. The creature had come to the wrong area. He slowly approached the tree the

Screamer landed upon. Damien guessed that it had spotted the wires Peter set up and was intelligent enough to bypass them by going through the trees. As he got closer to the tree, his heart skipped a beat and started to pound. Something had stepped out from behind the tree, but it wasn't the Screamer. It was the Alpha. Damien aimed his pistol with lightning speed and prepared to pull the trigger.

"Fire that weapon and I will leave you with two corpses to mourn over before you can even get halfway back to attempt a rescue." The Alpha's smile was apparent in the glow of his coat.

"What do you want?" Damien asked, not wavering with his weapon in the slightest.

"Your death. All of your deaths actually. Not yet, though. There are big events to come. Ones that will bring you to your knees. You and your entire race will beg me for death. However, I won't give you the release I was denied. I have spent millennia planning my revenge. I want you to witness it all come to fruition. I want you to feel like you have a chance to save those you love, to save your race. Sadly, that will never be the case. Your friend will be here soon, but he'll be safe. Don't repeat any of what just happened. I'll kill him if you do."

"You're sick," Damien growled, glaring at the hooded Prisoner.

"Your race was first." The Alpha smiled and blurred backward into the darkness, leaving Damien shaking with his thoughts. He didn't have a clue what the Alpha meant by any of it, and the feeling of being so close to death and helpless shook him to his core. He lowered his weapon, and the minutes passed as he stared into the darkness where the Alpha had disappeared. A hand lightly settled on his shoulder and he jumped.

"Whoa, just coming to switch with you." JD laughed but then stopped as he saw the look on Damien's face. "What happened?"

"Nothing," Damien immediately said. "Just tired."

JD's face showed amusement. "Well, you can go back and get rest now, bro. I have this until Peter switches shifts with me."

"Right," he said. Fear stirred within him, but he knew couldn't say a word. All he could do was let things go as they were and hope for the best. "Wake us up if there's anything too much for you to handle."

"If I do that, you'll both have a great night's sleep," JD replied. "I got this." He turned and began his watch.

Damien hesitantly went inside the hollow, where he saw Peter sound asleep. The space was dimly lit by a small electric lantern. He had lain down, but sleep was not quick to overcome him. The events and things that had been said the past day were swarming around. He didn't know how much time had passed before sleep finally forced itself upon him.

CHAPTER 12

Capital City

D amien woke up to the wonderful smell of food. He stirred from bed and looked around. No one was with him inside the hollow, and he noticed that all of their supplies were packed up in a corner. As he slowly rose from his bed, he turned and stared at it for a moment. He thought about being able to sleep in his home world after everything was accomplished. For a brief moment, he felt the deep longing to be home with those he loved.

The smell of food interrupted his contemplation, and he proceeded to walk out of the hollow to make sure his team was unharmed. To his surprise, there was a pile of Screamers near the entrance of the hollow. JD and Peter seemed to have been busy throughout the night, Damien thought. He then realized that he hadn't been woken up by either of them to perform another watch. He hoped that they were rested enough for the day ahead.

As he walked around the pile of dead Prisoners, he noticed Peter. He was hunched over a small fire. With a small stone over the top of it, he was cooking something he had caught. The world they were in had its own flora and fauna, and although the plant and animal life was less prevalent than that on their home world, Damien noticed that it had a slight resemblance to some from home.

Damien approached Peter. "Where did you get the game?"

"Oh, well, I went out scouting and found a small stream about a quarter mile away," Peter replied. "On the edge of the perimeter JD scouted."

"Good job, Pete, but don't you think the smell will attract Prisoners?"

"Where do you think that pile of Screamers came from?" he said, pointing at it.

"It would be dangerous if more than just those were attracted."

"That's why JD has been on lookout to make sure we have time to prepare for anything that thinks to steal our breakfast."

Damien thought the pile accumulated overnight, but according to what Peter said, it must have accumulated more recently. The forest steadily filled with more light as time progressed through the early morning.

"Where's JD?"

Peter took a bite of the cooked game and looked upward. "He's climbing the top of the tree to see what's ahead of us."

Damien looked up and noticed a small figure high up in the tree. It must be JD, he figured. JD moved behind one of the tree's massive branches and was no longer visible. Suddenly, he leaped from the tree and started free falling. Damien saw that an elastic safety cord was attached to JD's body, and he quickly fell toward the camp. Before Peter noticed his falling teammate, JD skillfully dropped in front of Peter and snatched from his hand the cooked game he was about to bite. Peter jumped and swiped at JD, but the cord had pulled him up to a nearby branch. He looked up to JD, who was a few feet above him, and pulled out a small, handmade blowgun loaded with a tranquilizer dart.

"Give it back, JD!"

"Don't you dare, Peter!"

"Then give it back."

JD brought the meat to his mouth and took a bite. "No," he replied around a mouthful of fish.

"Okay," Peter said, forming a grin. "You asked for it!" He took a deep breath and blew the dart at JD's neck.

It connected, and JD soon became sluggish and lost consciousness, falling from his perch. The cooked game fell from his hand, and Peter caught it. He resumed eating while JD hung overhead. Damien looked on in astonishment.

"Why did you do that?" Damien asked.

"Well, what I made had low potency. That's the only reason I used it on him. He won't be out long, but I can get him down."

Peter reached for his belt and pulled out his knife. He turned toward JD, aimed at the rope, and launched the knife into the air. The knife severed the rope, and JD began to fall. Damien, standing under his friend, caught him and set him down easy. After a minute, JD became conscious again and let out a moan. He looked over at Peter.

"Peter, you got me good, and that means that the payback will be good."

Peter took another bite of the meat. "Have fun with that."

"Yeah, I will."

The men gathered their supplies and resumed their journey.

"What did you see, JD?" Damien asked. "And where did you get that gear?"

"I mostly saw trees, but I noticed a large city ahead. It's not much on the horizon, but it's obvious that it is our destination. As for the gear, it's been in my bag. One of the days you were in the hospital I went and talked to Frank. He gave me this new gear to field test, and since I had the time this morning, I wanted to test it."

"Ah, I gotcha," Damien answered. "Sorry about losing the rope."

"That's fine. I saved enough for one more use. It's meant to be disposable."

As they moved toward their destination, terrifying roars shook the forest. Damien stopped and focused on the sounds. The men were able to discern that the roars came from two entities, and judging from the intensity of the roars, they were probably from Nightmare Prisoners. The team did not hesitate in moving forward at a faster rate, and each was fully alert.

The roars were sporadic, and after vigilantly moving for a few hours, it was recognized that the roars were moving around them and getting slightly louder. Eventually, the roars ceased for a time.

In a calm voice, Peter spoke. "They're close. We need to come up with a plan. If those roars are really from Nightmare Prisoners, we will have our hands full. We have only dealt with one at a time, but we may have to deal with two or more." He then had a smirk as he looked skyward. "I have an idea."

"What is it?" Damien and JD said in unison, eager to hear options.

"I've been looking around this forest, and I noticed that almost every branch of each tree connects to another. I say we climb them and continue from there. If things go well, we might be able to take care of our new friends as they search for us below." JD smiled at the notion of sniping.

Peter went to the base of one of the nearby trees and started climbing, and Damien and JD followed after him. The tree was so large that the bark acted as holds. It took a while to scale the tree and go out on one of its branches. It was enormous under their feet and shot forward to the nearest tree, intersecting with its branches. This continued with each tree for as far as they could see, with countless limbs.

Within an hour, they crossed many trees, and two ferocious roars were heard from the forest floor. The team peered over the edge of the branch and saw two large Prisoners walking on the forest floor. Both looked different from other Prisoners. Their body form was more bizarre, and they were chained together at their wrists by a very large chain. The creatures approached the base of the tree the team was on and looked upward.

"They're following our scent," Damien observed. "JD, fire a test round."

"I wonder which one of us smells best to them," he responded as he brought his sniper up and positioned himself to fire.

He fired a round from his sniper rifle at one of them, but it ricocheted off the armor that covered its face and into a nearby tree. The Prisoner grunted and glanced upward, catching sight of the squad. The Prisoners then knew the team's exact location.

A barrage of bullets rained down upon the pair, but it soon became apparent that neither sustained any damage. Both gave a toothy grin and continued to stare at the team. Suddenly, a grenade fell between the two. One of the Prisoners acted quickly and used the chain to propel its companion onto a tree, where it latched on with enormous claws and immediately pulled the other up the tree with it. Both escaped the exploding grenade. The two then started using that method to climb the tree and reach the team. The men looked on in surprise as the Prisoners came closer, ripped bark falling to the ground below from the speed and force of their climb.

"Oh, come on!" JD shouted. "How is that fair?"

He stood and darted to the next trees by way of the branches. Damien and Peter followed close behind.

Peter yelled at Damien, who was running ahead of him. "Can I have one as a pet?"

In bewilderment, Damien replied back. "If you can capture one, sure, but don't include me."

"Awesome! I'll call him Booskahkah."

The Prisoners eventually reached the same height as the team as they reached another tree. As the creatures gave chase to close the distance, the branches swayed beneath their stampeding weight. Damien soon came up with an idea as he ran with his team to the next trunk.

"Peter, get rid of this branch and drop them! They're closing in fast, so we don't have much time. Enough drop distance should do something to them."

"Aye, aye, Captain!"

Peter dashed ahead of Damien and pulled out a strange grenade. The Prisoners were barreling toward them from an adjacent tree. Peter pushed a button on the device as his friends passed him, and placed it where the branch connected to the tree. The grenade detonated, and a sphere of white particles exploded from it, expanding outward and into the branch beneath it. As the remains of the wood reformed in the sphere, Peter loosed another particle grenade into the pool of swirling dust, detonating another disintegrating sphere and deepening the hole. After it detonated, the branch heaved, splintering under its own weight. Peter produced an average fragmentation grenade, pulling the pin and tossing it toward the pit in the branch. It dropped to the bottom as he bolted for the next branch while the Prisoners pulled each other onto the branch.

Moments later, a loud explosion was heard, and the large branch snapped with a thundering bang, causing its occupants to plummet to the ground. Unexpectedly, each Prisoner fell on one side of a lower branch, and their chain wrapped around the top, leaving them to hang helplessly. The long fall snapped their wrists and dislocated their shoulders. The monsters were unable to move and roared in utter agony.

"I caught both of them!" Peter said gleefully as he stopped to look upon his handiwork. "How do we get them back home? I wonder if I can get them housebroken."

"We don't have time, Peter!" Damien yelled. "We need to focus on getting to the tower!"

"Fine, but we're picking them up on the way back. You said I could keep them if I caught them."

JD walked behind Damien. "They're not cats, Peter," he said.

"That's not the point," he replied. "I know I joke a lot about Prisoners and them being pets, but I truly believe something can be done with them."

"All right, whatever. Let's get going. We have a little bit more to go before we reach the capital city. Stay alert. We don't know what else could spring up."

The three began navigating through the tree tops. After spending hours upon hours speed walking through the trees, they caught sight of the city at a distance. It wouldn't be long before they were there. Upon reaching the end of the forest nearing the end of the day, the team came to a massively open area. The city was located in the middle and was dark against the light of the invisible setting sun.

"It's going to take a while to cross that plain between us and the city. Let's make camp up here tonight," Damien said as he dropped his bag down and walked to the edge of the branch.

"Sounds like a plan!" JD sounded off. "I'm going to see if I can make radio contact with Josiah. If he is close enough, that is."

"Good idea," Damien said as he stared at the grand cluster of buildings in the distance. As the surroundings grew darker, a green glow began emanating from the city. It was a beautiful sight, like a shining cluster of emeralds just waiting to be discovered.

"I wonder if there is a way in there to bring you back." His voice was low and his mind filled with thought. Before he could let those thoughts consume him, he was saved.

"I know it's got to hurt," Peter said as he stepped up beside his friend. "To have someone you care about so much snatched away from you and there was nothing you could have done. However, even knowing that, we blame ourselves."

"I should have been able to do something, though."

"You can't prevent what you don't know will happen." Peter paused for a few moments as he contemplated the next words he would speak. "You know, I blamed myself for his death. My brother came here and was killed within a couple of weeks. He was the one I looked up to and my rock whenever life would knock me down. Yet I let him come here and never once tried to stop him. I feel as though he would have stayed had I said something. It took time and meeting new friends for me to realize that it wasn't my fault. He died doing what he wanted and protecting people. Unlike me, though, you get a chance to save her. I never had that chance. Now I'm not saying I had it worse. When I got the news, it was absolute. He was dead, and that was reality. You get a chance that many only wish and dream they could have. Don't take that for granted. Stay happy and positive for her until you bring her home. Even if there isn't a way to do it here, we'll do it on Earth. No matter what."

Damien looked at his friend, who had kept such a calm and serious tone. All the words he had spoken were true. As Damien thought back on his actions, he realized that he had acted as though Moriah was already dead. He never realized that he had already thought of her fate as such when it was never the case. He looked at his friend and felt a warmth of comfort. Peter had grown so much since he had met him. He had been in such a dark place but came out as one of the happiest people he knew.

"Thanks, bro," Damien said as a tear dropped from his eye. It was something he had needed. Peter patted him on his back and walked to JD, who had been setting up a secure area to sleep. He had no luck reaching Josiah and assumed they were either out of range or the signal was being jammed. Damien took one last look at the city and thought of her, her smile and the way she made him feel. "Just wait for me." He smiled and walked to his friend. They spent a few hours of the night swapping stories from their lives. Afterward they went to sleep, with one keeping watch, rotating turns throughout the night. Thanks to his friends, Damien finally slept in peace.

The team got up as light started to break the sky open. They packed up and safely climbed down to begin their walk across the lush plain of grass between them and their final destination. It took a couple of hours of walking before they arrived at a long stretch of bridge that led all the way to the city. Damien observed the city; it was larger than he expected it would be and larger than it had seemed from up in the tree. It had small buildings on the outskirts, but the buildings grew larger the closer they were to the center of the city. The tower that was the team's destination was at the center, and the key that would end the war was at the top of it. The team did not know what horrors could be awaiting them.

The appearance of the city did not give off an ominous feel. A large canyon circled it, and many rivers flowed off its edges and into a deep abyss. Four bridges crossed the canyon, one for each side. It was a brilliant city, and Damien was saddened by the realization that it would soon be destroyed by nukes. He was suddenly startled by a familiar voice in his ear.

"Damien," Josiah exclaimed, "I've been trying to get a hold of you for a while. We were beginning to think you were killed."

Damien chuckled. "Aww, you care about us. We miss you too, bud."

"What's your location?"

"We are presently at the edge of the city. Where are you? We tried to get a hold of you but got nothing."

"We've just come across a large branch that fell from one of the trees. I guess it fell due to a past storm or something. Systems have been acting up, so that is probably why you couldn't reach us."

Damien smiled as he listened. "A large branch, huh? Look upward."

After a few seconds, Josiah shouted in surprise. "Woah! How did you manage that?"

"Peter was actually the one who pulled it off. A couple new grenades to dig a deep hole then a normal one to blow it apart. Their weight helped as well. Be sure not to kill them. Peter wants them as pets. With their wrists and shoulders damaged, they shouldn't be able to escape and cause any problems."

"Understood. We're a little ways behind you. I'll go ahead and call evac and tell them to get ready. Since you're so far ahead, it'll take quite some time to catch up. Is there a place we can use as an extraction point?"

Damien peered at the city. "Yes. There are four bridges around the city. The front bridge, it'll be the first you see, would be a good extraction point. You'll see it when you exit the forest."

"Got it."

"All right. Unless there is an emergency, I would like radio silence. We are going to infiltrate the city and tower, and we need to use as much stealth as we can."

"Radio if you need backup. Good luck."

"Thanks."

Damien turned off his communication with Josiah and looked out at the city.

JD spoke up. "Well, I'm ready when you two are. I won't be able to rappel down from the tower because my line is too short." He glared at Peter.

"That's all right, buddy," Peter replied with a grin. "You can rappel down with me."

"You don't have the gear."

"Oh, well we can just walk back down."

"I'm sure we can get picked up at the top," Damien said. "The jets should have hover capabilities."

"And if they don't?" JD questioned.

"Then we find another way. Either way, we're getting home with that key."

Damien turned his focus to the bridge that was before him and estimated that it was about a half-mile long. The steel-gray bridge had pillars on the sides, and black lines were prominently displayed. The lines were a complete grid, a different design from the other architectural features Damien had seen on the planet. When the first step was taken onto the bridge, it reacted. The black lines immediately shifted to a glowing green. The bridge separated into multiple parts on its side and began taking on a new appearance. The parts shifted into pillars, with certain parts glowing more brilliantly than others. The men looked on in astonishment.

Once the transformation was complete, the men proceeded forward. A hologram materialized in front of them and displayed what appeared to be a map of the city.

"What is your destination?" the hologram asked.

"The main tower," Damien replied without hesitation. "We aim to retrieve the key to the portal."

There was a brief pause before the hologram replied, "Request confirmed. Destination, control center, marked. Please proceed."

The hologram vanished into the surface at his feet after that, and the once glowing green lines became dark again. Subsequently, a pulse of complex, broken grid work shot forward across the bridge, and a white light signaling the path to their destination was periodically generated.

"Well, at least we won't have to stop and ask for directions," JD said.

"Let's go," Damien replied, and the men began their walk toward the city.

When they reached the halfway point of the bridge, which did not take them long, Peter walked over to the side of the bridge and peered over it. Shimmering water poured down into the abyss below. Mist filled the area and seemed like a ring of clouds surrounding the pedestal of earth on which the city sat.

"I think I found my summer condo, Damien!" Peter said.

Damien laughed. "You can have the canyon. I'll have the city."

"You know what I meant."

"Be more clear next time. I have dibs on the city now," Damien snickered.

"I say the first one who gets there has dibs on it!" JD yelled, running toward the city gates.

Damien turned to Peter. "Do you have another tranquilizer dart?"

"Way ahead of you," he said, inserting a dart. He took aim and fired. The dart flew through the air and hit the back of JD's neck.

"Screw you, Peter!" JD said before collapsing.

"Will it be easy to wake him up?" Damien asked.

"Yeah. Same as last time."

The two both glanced at each other and started racing to the city. Damien was the first to reach the gate, with Peter being a close second. Both were out of breath. Peter wasn't happy about losing the race, but he was glad that he wasn't like JD, lying on the bridge. Soon JD woke up and made his way to the city gates. He didn't like the fact that he didn't reach the city first, but he admired how quick Peter was in his thinking. Damien greeted him when he approached them.

"Don't worry, JD. You can rent it out anytime, for a price."

JD chuckled. "Whatever. Let's just get this over with."

The large gate before them had a huge hole at its center. It could not be good news, Damien thought. With his pistol in hand, he peered through the hole, then proceeded to lead them through it. The entire city seemed dark and void of life, but it lit up in response to their presence. Everything within the city seemed like something humans would theoretically construct. Lights made of steel lined the roadways. Automatic doors and windows that tinted in response to light were a feature on every building they came across. The buildings were very tall, and some were connected via tubes. Damien guessed that they were walkways of some sort. The tubes sometimes crossed overhead, with flat walkways and clear sides. There was no sign of debris on the streets, as if they had always been cleaned. A door opened near the team, similar to how the door to the armory opened.

"This is pretty amazing," Peter said. "It's as if we've traveled into the future in a time machine."

"Stay focused. We have a mission to complete," Damien responded. The men moved toward their destination.

"I was thinking," Peter began. "The computer said that our destination is the control tower."

"So?" Damien replied. "What are you thinking about?"

"What all do you think it could control?"

"Maybe just functions of this city. Maybe more. I have no idea." The thought of it possibly controlling more than just the city was a spark of hope. It made him wonder if somewhere in the city was a way to bring back Moriah.

"Maybe. I've been thinking about something else. Doesn't the city seem like something we as humans would be capable of making in the future? There are uncanny resemblances to the architectural concepts in our world."

"Yes, I've been thinking along those lines."

"Yeah. There's a lot about this place that we still don't understand, but I'm increasingly getting the feeling that the minds behind all this are similar to us in some fashion."

"Me, too. We can talk about it later, though. Key first."

The team moved cautiously and silently through the city streets. Damien estimated that it would take close to an hour to reach the base of the exceedingly high tower. Suddenly, the team heard an explosion ahead of them. The ground shook beneath their feet and made each of them glance at each other. They all felt that the cause of the hole in the city gate was about to greet them. Their presence was revealed thanks to the reaction of the city upon their arrival.

"We have to move fast and remain alert. That wasn't too far away," Damien announced. "JD, move through the rooftops and get a good view of what's ahead of us."

"Got it," JD immediately said. He dashed to the nearest building and ducked inside. It didn't take him long to reach the rooftop and call out to Damien. "Hey, the heights of the buildings increase as we move toward the center. I'm not sure whether I'll be able to keep jumping from building to building or not."

"I know," Damien replied. "All of the buildings have windows at the same level and are relatively close. There's a ledge on each one, so go about carefully moving from ledge to ledge. Switch your headset on and set it to local and test it. I want to see if we can at least communicate."

JD nodded and began stealthily moving down rooftops, searching for hostiles. The local channel worked, and they could talk as they pushed forward.

Damien turned to Peter. "Peter, you'll follow me. Your shotgun will provide great close-quarters protection as we move through the city. Stay close. Understood?"

"Yup," Peter answered. He crouched low to the side of a building and moved along its edge so he couldn't be seen as easily.

Damien spoke through the headset. "What's the status report?"

"I really have to pee," JD replied. "Do you think there's a bathroom in the tower?"

"Status report, JD."

"That is the status report. I really have to—stop where you are, guys!"

Damien and Peter came to a halt. "What is it, JD?"

"A Prisoner is closing in on you," JD communicated through the headset. "It's two streets up and about to come around a corner."

Damien scanned the building tops and found JD in the opening of a window. Then he was forced to turn his attention to a bulky Prisoner. It was heavily armored and had a height of about twelve feet. The Prisoner did not immediately notice them, so Damien grabbed Peter and pulled him to the nearest building to hide from its sight.

Damien whispered into the communicator. "What is it doing, JD?"

"It's doing what I want to do pretty badly right now," JD replied.

"What?"

"I'm joking. It sniffed the air and turned its head toward your building. It's running toward it now. Get out of there."

Damien felt the ground vibrate from the beast's steps. He scanned the room he and Peter were in and saw a type of staircase in the far corner. He signaled to Peter to take it. As the two made their way up, the ground vibrations stopped.

JD yelled through the communicator. "It jumped toward your building!"

Before Damien could react, the wall behind him was broken down, and the Prisoner crashed into the room. It darted past Damien and Peter and out the other end of the building.

"I lost visual," JD announced. "However, the next couple of streets on the other side of your location are filled with dust."

Damien reached the rooftop of the building and observed the dust for himself. JD was right. A building had collapsed from the impact of the Prisoner. The dust undulated, and soon, another building collapsed. Damien realized that it was making another pass for its prey.

"Run, Peter! Jump to the next building!"

As soon as he gave the command, the building shook again. He looked back to where they had entered the rooftop and saw that the building had started to collapse. He sprinted toward the next building where Peter was running to. His heart pounded as the ground slowly fell from under his feet. It was collapsing piece by piece, quickly catching up with him. When he made it to the edge, he jumped and rolled onto the next building. It wasn't over yet. The building he and Peter were on shook.

"JD! Can you find a way to take care of it?"

"The only potentially lethal points I noticed were the eyeholes on its helmet. If you can get it into the open and briefly keep it still, I can line up a shot."

"Be ready," Damien said.

He found JD in another open window. This time he had moved five buildings toward the control center.

"Peter, we need to get down ASAP and move past JD." He pointed in JD's direction.

Peter shrugged indicating that he didn't know how to get down. The building began to collapse, and they both moved toward the next building. Suddenly, the building stopped falling and was sitting at an angle.

"Are you thinking what I'm thinking?" Damien asked Peter.

"Ride down?" Peter said, grinning.

Damien responded with a similar grin. The collapsing rubble from the rooftop had started again but at a slower pace. Their side of the building was smooth and allowed for them to slide down it with ease. Damien and Peter slid down the side, dodging the occasional flying debris. The Prisoner soon appeared from the chaos, running toward them on the ground below. As they reached the height of the Prisoner, it also reached them. They both leapt off the wall, over the Prisoner, and onto the ground. The Prisoner built up so much momentum that it continued through the next four buildings. They made it out of the destruction and onto the street, sprinting in JD's direction. After passing a few buildings, the Prisoner burst out in front of them. Debris flew overhead.

"Die, Creators!" it roared.

It leaned forward and began rushing at them. They had nowhere to go.

"Boom," JD announced over the communicator. He fired several rounds from his sniper rifle, piercing the Prisoner's right eye. Each round could be heard hitting the inside of the metal helmet. It slammed into the ground as it collapsed and slid a few feet before rumbling to a stop. Blood spewed from its mouth and left a streak across the pavement.

"Thanks, JD," Damien said. He was nearly out of breath. "You can join us now."

Once JD rejoined, the Prisoner began moving. It slowly lifted its head from the pavement. The men jumped back and fired their guns into its eye sockets. It let out a final roar and finally died. Suddenly, the city filled with roars and screams. The roar of the Prisoner they had killed triggered a dangerous event. Damien set his sights on their destination. He looked to the ground as it lit up once more and another pulse led toward their target.

"Run," he said to his teammates, and all three began sprinting toward the tower.

The base of the tower was soon in front of them, and the entrance could be seen. Damien estimated that they would reach it within a few minutes. He then thought about the potential danger upon entering the tower. There may be Prisoners inside, he thought. As he pondered this, a screech was heard. A Screamer. Damien came to an immediate halt, and the Screamer shot past him, crashing into a building to his left. Peter fired his shotgun at the creature before Damien could lift his pistol to aim. It fell lifelessly to the ground. Other Screamers and Slashers swarmed out of the building ahead of them. Many fell from JD's excellent sniping. Anything that approached them had their vitals slashed by Damien's knife. Peter used his shotgun to take care of all of the Prisoners that tried to attack them from behind.

The ground began shaking again, and multiple Nightmare Prisoners appeared, breaking from nearby buildings, which caused them to topple over. The team focused on the path to the tower. The pulsing light they had been following maneuvered itself around the dead bodies and debris that increasingly filled the streets. They eventually made it to the tower, and Prisoners were right behind them. Unexpectedly, all of the Prisoners started to drop to the ground. The men looked up and saw what appeared to be exceedingly large gun turrets on the sides of the tower. Each turret lit up as it fired on the prisoners, resounding with a barrage of muffled explosions. Each shot was precise and disintegrated the target, resulting in an instant kill of floating, white particles. Soon, not a single hostile moved in the streets.

Damien slowed to a stop at the steps that led to the tower's door. He again glanced at the weapons overhead that saved them. He did not understand why they had been spared. As he approached the door, he noticed a monitor to the right of it. There was a message displayed.

Damien read the monitor aloud. "It says that the area is now secure." He then looked through a nearby window. "And it doesn't seem that anything is broken inside to hint at a Prisoner break-in. Regardless, let's remain alert."

"Props to any Prisoner that does manage a break-in," JD laughed, slightly out of breath.

Damien searched for the door's handle and realized it didn't have one. There was nothing to press to open the door either. He attempted to push the door open, but it didn't budge. He looked back at the monitor and saw that it displayed an onscreen button with the term "scan" over it. He pressed the button and a green line appeared. It flashed over the team from head to toe and vanished afterward. The door opened, revealing the inside of the building. The men didn't bother wondering why they were given access. They looked inside and found a very dark lobby. Before stepping inside, a loud noise was heard overhead. Fragments of the building rained down around them. They looked up and saw that one of the weapons that had protected them had a street pole running through it. It was no doubt inoperable, Damien thought. He turned to see where the street pole came from.

Standing in the center of the street was a monstrous Prisoner. Its mouth was filled with large fangs, and it looked almost thirty feet tall. It could easily destroy the surrounding buildings, and based on the destroyed turret, it was also capable of destroying machines. Peter and JD ran inside the lobby before Damien, and he followed after them. They came to a staircase and started going up. Another crashing sound came from outside, and sparks rained down.

"We've seen how bad those things are, so taking the elevator isn't a good idea," JD said. He ran and reached the landing of the first floor. "I hope that the turrets can take care of that thing before it takes care of this building."

Peter slowed to a halt. "Wait. There's an elevator?"

"This is a tower, after all, Pete," Damien answered. "There must be one, but it's not safe to take it."

The men continued moving. "I need more exercise anyway," Peter said.

Damien led the team through the tower, searching for a way up. They soon found a room with a spiral staircase. From the look of it, it led all the way to the top of the spire. They immediately took the staircase and began moving upward.

"Can we have lunch break when we're halfway?" Peter asked jokingly, noticing the height to which the stairs rose.

"Yeah," JD replied. "Better idea, let's go back down and invite Mr. KillsEverything and see if he'd be willing to join. I bet he'll be happy you asked."

146

"It doesn't seem that this place has been breached at all in the time it's been here," Peter stated, leaving JD's response alone. "Why are Prisoners destroying it now?"

"They have something to chase after now?"

"Makes sense," Peter replied.

JD sighed. "Look, it seems that the Prisoners have been alone for quite some time, and now we're here. It wouldn't be surprising if their first instinct is to track down and kill whatever comes up. They'll probably do whatever it takes to accomplish that."

They were getting closer to the top of the tower. Even though fatigue was starting to set in, they pushed on.

"How are we going to know which room contains the key?" JD asked. "Will there be only one room at the top?"

"I don't know," Damien answered. "We'll have to search everywhere when we reach the top."

"You should see if you can contact Josiah," JD said. "We want those jets to be ready, so tell him we'll be done in about half an hour."

"It will be longer than half an hour. This tower is incredibly tall, and we still have to find the key. I'll still call him, though." Damien turned on his headset to Josiah's channel. "Josiah, can you hear me?"

A moment of static was followed by a reply. "Yes, I hear you. You sound like you're out of breath."

"Are you at the bridge?"

"I'm near it, yes," his voice sounded a bit odd, but Damien disregarded it.

"Do you see the tower in the center of the city?"

"Yes, I do. It's hard to miss. We heard some commotion going on over there."

"We decided to have a bit of fun while sightseeing. We're inside the tower, presently moving toward the top. Once we reach the top, we'll search for the key. Call for the jets, and meet us there. We certainly don't want to go back down."

"Understood," Josiah said. "I'll see you there."

Damien turned his headset off once again and realized that Josiah said that he had heard commotion, but Damien wasn't hearing it. To Damien's surprise, it had become eerily quiet, and he was afraid of what that meant. He turned his focus upward on making it to the top. It took the team quite some time to reach the top, but they finally made it to the end of the stairs. The stairs led to a hallway with large doors at its end. The walls of the hallway were lined with the familiar glowing green lines.

"Well, I believe this answers your question, JD."

"Indeed it does."

"Let's do this," Peter said. He walked forward with his shotgun ready to be fired at any moment.

They approached the doors, and each shone very brightly. A voice arose from them.

"State your purpose," the voice said.

Before Damien could reply, Peter stepped forward and bowed. "We come for the key, O Great Wizard."

The men were suddenly scanned like they had been at the entrance of the tower; however, the scan appeared to search the entire area, including the hallway and stairs.

"Multiple hostiles are moving toward your present location. Access to the control room is granted. Lock and defense systems will activate after you have entered the room. Welcome back."

"Moving toward us? What do you mean?" Damien asked.

"Welcome back?" Peter asked in confusion.

The doors opened. "Your questions will be answered momentarily. Please proceed."

The doors closed behind them, and they examined the control room. It contained a round, mechanical table at its center, and a hologram of the portal hovered over it. The walls were windows that revealed the entire landscape. Damien noticed a chair, turned away from them, at the front of the table. He slowly approached it and looked to see if it was empty. To his surprise, it had an occupant. It wasn't a living occupant, however. It was a skeleton dressed in strange military garb. Based on its various features, it looked to be a human skeleton. The team was quite surprised at the sight. While JD and Peter continued to examine the skeleton, Damien addressed the automated voice. "We need the key to turn off the portal on our world."

"Your presence here indicates that you are already in possession of one key. If you wish to close the portal, you will need to shut it down from here."

"We can't shut it down from here. We need to go home."

"The only way that would be possible is to merge the present key with your key. It will result in a meltdown, and the portal will collapse. Your race will not be able to come back and inherit their past."

Damien was impatient, "I need that key now. Where is it?"

"The answer you seek is behind you."

Damien turned around and stood before the seated skeleton. He examined it more closely. A small book was held in its boney hands. He gently picked it up. To have his questions answered, he opened the book and began to skim through. He knew there wasn't enough time to read the entire thing. Page after page he turned until he reached the end of the small journal.

All of the civilians have successfully evacuated, and all that remained were soldiers who guarded the portal. They were waiting for me. "Give them the green light, computer." When the soldiers received the notification, they went through the portal. I was then the only man in the world. I initiated the shutdown of the portal, and it soon vanished. There were two lights on the table in front of me, one red and one green. The green light indicated that the portal on our world's side was still active. It became red after a few moments. When it did, I turned the portal on once more. This left only one green light, and that was mine. I accomplished my mission. As I finish my story, I cannot help but wonder what will become of this world. I continue to think about what the C-ZERO said. I am not worried, however. We are a strong-willed race, and we will certainly win. For the future humanity that finds this place, I have placed the key in the locked compartment. The access code is . . .

"Gone," Damien sighed. "Part of the page is gone."

CHAPTER 13

The Escape

Damien stared at the part of the page that should have held the code. It seemed to have been ripped away. Time was running short, and they didn't have time to search everywhere.

"Damien," JD began, "It's been a while, and the jets still haven't shown up."

"Long-range sensors show primitive aircraft inbound," the computer announced.

"You're primitive," Peter mumbled.

"Unidentified human inbound as well," the computer replied.

Damien and the others stared at each other with uneasy confusion. He quickly put the ancient journal into his pack and turned with his team to face the door, waiting to see who would come in. Moments later the door opened, and it was Josiah who entered the room with his pistol at his side. It immediately became apparent that there was something different about him. He had an ominous presence. Something was wrong with him, and Peter was the first to approach.

"What's the matter, buddy? You don't look too—"

A bang resounded throughout the room that made every breath hold, and Peter fell to the floor with a thud. Damien immediately threw up his pistol and aimed it at Josiah, who was aiming his pistol back at him, unwavering.

"Peter always talked too much," Josiah said with a grin. "I thought it would be a good idea to shut him up before he got carried away."

JD immediately went to Peter's side and started dressing the wound.

"JD!" Damien yelled. "Get Peter out to the side balcony and wait for the jets. There is one right over there. Nurse his wounds as best as you can. I'll take care of this."

JD lifted and carried Peter without saying a word and left the room. Peter was clutching his chest, and his eyes squeezed shut in pain.

"That could be a fatal wound," Josiah declared. "You might want to have it treated immediately if you're even able to save him at all." His voice became sinister.

"Why are you doing this?" Damien replied, still aiming his pistol at him. "Do you think your sister would approve of your actions? You know she wouldn't."

"Let's just say that he's not himself at the moment," said a mysterious voice behind Josiah. "But nice try pulling the family card. It really hurt him on the inside."

Damien's heart pounded as he saw the Alpha step out from behind Josiah.

"What did you do?" Damien yelled as his aim focused on the hooded man.

"Does it matter? It's done."

Josiah rested his pistol to his side when the Alpha stood beside him.

"What have you done to him?" Damien questioned, his finger shaking on the trigger in rage.

"I was simply trying to become acquainted. I tapped into his neural system with an old device my creators had made at one point. Oh, that primitive weapon will be of no use to you, so you might as well put it away. I've warned you once about this."

Damien pulled the trigger to shoot the enemy, but something unexpected happened. He was shocked to see that the Alpha caught the bullet in the palm of its gloved hand. The being smiled back at him, amused by his surprise.

"As I've said, that weapon is of no use to you. Put it away. There already will be consequences."

Seeing that his weapon was indeed useless in direct contact, he placed it back in its holster. He stared at the enemy, a hand instinctively resting on the grip, waiting for a chance of surprise.

"What do you want?" Damien asked, resisting the urge to unleash his whole magazine onto the man.

"I simply wish to talk."

"Just like you wished to talk to Peter and Josiah?!" He quickly looked to make sure JD had left the room and then adjusted his attention back to his friend and his enemy.

Damien's reply gave the Alpha pause.

"You care so much about such meaningless lives. If you knew what your ancestors did in the past, you would see my side in a much different light."

Damien was furious at how his friends were nothing in the eyes of the enemy, but he couldn't expect more. The enemy was merciless and heartless.

"How do you justify making Josiah shoot Peter?"

"It wasn't an easy task, mind you. Even with the control over him I have currently, his struggle against shooting his new friend was great and almost admirable, even to me. You can't even imagine how much he broke at the mention of what his sister would think of him. I shot your friend to get him out of the way. I am sure your comrades would do anything to protect you. Yes, his wound may be fatal, but fatality is the fruit of war. That is how it shall be, for your species, at least." The Alpha chuckled.

"Why do all this?"

"I wish I had the precious time to tell you," the man said, raising his hand to point. "but it seems that we have run out of time."

The Alpha pointed to the balcony door, and Damien could see their jet through the small, adjacent windows. It was an aircraft like he had never seen before.

"Perhaps you'll make it back before the first wave of nightmare hits," The Alpha said with a grin. "I have a ride to catch, myself."

The hooded figure turned to leave but paused and turned back around behind Josiah. Josiah didn't budge throughout the entire conversation, but a tear that had run down his cheek leaving a trail of sorrow and regret.

"Oh, and you can have your friend back. He is no longer of any use to me." He reached out and grabbed Josiah's head, swiftly snapping his neck. "I told you there would be consequences."

"No!" Damien yelled, releasing all the air from his lungs as he grabbed his pistol and fired at the Alpha, who quickly fled and disappeared from the room. Damien ran over to Josiah, whose body lay still on the floor, and checked to see if he was alive. His eyes were open, and the light had faded. Sadness bit into Damien's heart, but he knew that he didn't have time to grieve. He lifted Josiah's body to carry him and made his way to the balcony where another pending sorrow was awaiting him. He noticed JD putting Peter into the jet on a stretcher. Damien's gut twisted itself into knots at the thought of his friend dying. It was already upside down from Josiah.

With Peter inside the jet, JD approached Damien, who was bringing Josiah's body to the jet. JD's eyes widened at the sight, but he didn't ask any questions. Just like Damien, he knew that there wasn't time for sadness. The time to break would have to come later.

"How's Peter?" Damien asked, raising his voice to overcome the roar of the jet.

"He's alive, but he needs medical treatment immediately," JD replied. "There seems to be another problem, though, and it's not about Pete."

"What's that?"

"We keep trying to get in touch with the base, but there's no response. We don't have the status of the nukes or anything."

Damien felt dread as he reflected on what the Alpha had told him. They had to move fast. He sprinted back to the control room, keeping an eye out for hostiles, and stood before the control table.

"Computer, where's the compartment with the deactivation key for my world's portal?"

"The compartment is located under the two green lights displaying the status of the portals."

Damien quickly searched and found the lights above the small compartment that held the key. He tried to open it, but it was locked. Attempt after attempt was futile.

"Open it," he demanded.

"A password is required. It may be found within this room. Without the password, I can't open the compartment."

"The password is gone! We need to get the key and get out of here now!"

"A password is required to receive the key."

"I'll just have to take it then," he said through clenched teeth.

Damien pulled out his rifle, took a few steps back, and took aim. He was going to get the key and get his friends home.

"The use of a weapon is not wise."

"I don't care. This is my mission, and I don't intend to fail. Human lives depend on it! She depends on it!"

He aimed at the compartment and pulled the trigger. The shot blew the metallic lid off of the compartment, and alarms began to sound. The computer issued a notification.

"Requirements for protocol met. Mass planetary evacuation in five minutes. Destination: Saturn."

Damien paid little attention to the computer's words. Rage and confusion filled him to the brim. All he could think of was the mission. He dashed to the compartment and grabbed the key, a stack of crystalized disks in a small, transparent casing. The disks rotated and changed colors, shifting black and green. He shoved the key in his pocket and ran back to the jet. JD was inside the jet waiting for Damien's return and was relieved to see his friend running back. Damien jumped aboard and quickly shut the door.

"Go!" Damien yelled. "We have to get back ASAP!"

"What's wrong?" JD replied as the jet turned and took off with force, pushing both into their seats.

"A massive Prisoner attack is being launched on our base, and since I took this code by force, there is a protocol to evacuate this planet to Saturn!" The reality of his words hit him. Moriah was possibly in danger. He held back a tear. "We have to get to Saturn."

"We will," JD said, trying to comfort him, "but let's focus on what's before us."

Damien nodded in agreement. Suddenly, he saw something fly by the jet, heading in the direction of the ancient city.

"Those are the nukes!" Damien said with fear in his voice. "They're early!"

"There's no escaping it. They were built to destroy the city and everything around it within a large radius. We won't have time to get away from those."

Damien and JD watched helplessly as the nuclear weapons traveled toward the city. After a moment, the weapons detonated and brought forth blinding light. The light eventually dissipated, and Damien looked out and saw something he couldn't believe. Formed over the city was a barrier of some kind. The light and energy from the nukes were absorbed and looked like a system of grid-like veins spreading over the dome. The sky began to turn blue, and the clouds turned white. Across the horizon in all directions, Damien saw that there were hundreds of metallic pods climbing into the sky. Each pod shone with light, a long blue stream connecting it to the ground. Each pod disappeared into its own misty, swirling portal. By the time everything was done, the barrier completely had absorbed the energy from the nuclear weapons, and a familiar sight greeted them: Haven resembled Earth completely. Even the sun was visible.

The events left Damien and JD without words. Each believed that they were both mere seconds from death, yet they were still alive with a mission to complete.

"I don't know how to react to all this."

"Me neither," Damien replied. He noticed the jet declining in altitude. "We may need to pilot the jet, though. I think our pilot just died of a heart attack."

"Yeah, good idea."

JD got up and entered the cockpit. A moment later the jet leveled out and the afterburners were enabled. The jet greatly increased in speed, pushing Damien deeply into his seat once more.

Damien turned on his headset. "Whenever I figure out the ETA to base, I'll let you know," JD said through the headset. "Is Peter still all right?"

Damien looked over Peter who was lying in front of him on a stretcher that had been secured. He was unconscious, and his chest wound was bandaged tightly. Blood steadily seeped through.

"Yeah, he's fine, but we have to hurry."

"Right. Hey, we might be dropping in a hot zone. If there's a large Prisoner attack, we're going to have to land dangerously close but safely to keep Peter out of harm's way."

"We'll survey the base before making any decisions. Let's just worry about getting there for now."

As they sped toward the base, Damien looked at his comrades in the back with him. One was unconscious, and the other was lifeless. Neither one deserved it. No one in the war deserved any of the pain, but reality didn't care. He was determined to end the war. He peered out and observed the landscape swiftly passing by.

"We'll get there in less than an hour. You should make preparations," JD announced.

Damien agreed and checked his inventory. While checking his ammunition, he thought about how he would get Peter and Josiah through the portal in case the base was being attacked. Time seemed to pass at an excruciatingly slow pace, and after what seemed like an eternity, he felt the aircraft start to slow down. They were making the approach.

"They were expecting us!" JD exclaimed as the jet began flying at a much slower speed as they neared the base's airspace. The jet angled upward. "There's long ranged Pulser energy firing at us. There isn't much, though, so I should be able to maneuver through all of them. Just hang on!"

JD piloted the jet to evade a barrage of energy shots coming from below, and Damien held onto Peter's stretcher to make sure he was kept in place. He looked over to Josiah's body to make sure it was still strapped in and safe. After a moment, the jet experienced an impact and started to slow down even more drastically.

"Our tail was hit," JD shouted. "I can see the base, though. This is going to be a rough landing."

Damien immediately took Peter from the stretcher and fastened him to one of the seats as best as he could.

"What's the situation at the base?" The jet was dropping rapidly at that point. "Where will we land?"

JD replied back instantly. "It doesn't look good. I'm aiming for just outside the portal facility. I can see several explosions, and there are multiple Nightmare Prisoners."

"How long until impact?" Damien yelled as the jet began to tremble violently.

"Now!" JD said, leaving the cockpit and fastening himself to one of the seats. He barely managed to secure himself before the jet crashed into the ground. The jet screeched as it slid across the ground.

When the jet came to a halt, Damien grabbed his pistol and shot a Slasher that had immediately ripped through the side of the jet. It collapsed at his feet, and he turned to JD while unfastening himself from his seat.

"Get Peter ready! I'll take Josiah and clear the area!"

Mere moments after leaving the jet, an energy shot from a Pulser met its mark and set the aircraft on fire. The men sprinted away, making as much distance from the jet as they could. The environment was filled with combat. Soldiers were everywhere, and Prisoners were decimating their ranks. Many tanks and vehicles were in shambles. A huge Nightmare Prisoner was near the crash site of Damien and JD's former jet, and Damien looked frantically for an escape route.

"JD! There's a door coming up. Follow me into it. We're going close to the portal."

Upon reaching the door, Damien busted it open. JD and Peter went in first. The Nightmare Prisoner noticed them and roared, turning to chase after them. Damien shut the door behind them, and they both ran down the hallway of the building. The door, along with the wall it was a part of, burst apart shortly after he closed it, and the Prisoner rushed down the hallway on all fours.

"Take a left!" Damien shouted. "Look for a familiar place so we can find the portal!"

After taking a left turn, they rushed to avoid being spotted a second time by the Prisoner. The beast rushed down the hallway without turning and kept running forward. They were safe for the moment.

The familiar hum came to Damien's ears, and he slowly came to a halt as he readjusted Josiah. "I hear the portal!" The humming was reverberating from down the hallway. "This way!"

He took the lead and eventually came to a door that led to the portal. The room revealed the large orb with its blue energy oscillating from its edges. Soldiers guarded the portal, which had additional soldiers coming through it. The roof began cracking as something was trying to get inside. A soldier who had just killed a Screamer noticed the men headed his way.

"The key is here!" the soldier yelled. "Get SF5-3 through the portal and retreat!" The soldier saw that they needed medical attention. "Have a medical team standing by!" The man came over and took Josiah from him and through the portal.

Damien turned to notice a familiar soldier engaged in hand-to-hand combat with a Slasher. It was Avery, and after quickly killing the Prisoner, he reiterated that everyone needed to retreat. Fellow soldiers assisted JD in getting Peter through the portal safely. After JD, Peter, and the soldiers safely went through the portal, it was Damien's turn to go through. He approached the portal, and Avery stepped up beside him. Damien's heart sank as he knew the events that would soon follow.

"It's time to leave," Avery said with a battle-worn grin.

Both men went through the portal and left the chaotic world behind. Damien opened his eyes and realized that he'd returned to the dome-shaped room. Wounded soldiers filled the area, and medics were frantically providing medical attention. He looked about for Peter and JD but could not find them. Josiah's body wasn't in sight either.

A scientist saw Damien and yelled to him from the bottom of the stairs. "Where's the key?"

"I have it right here," he said, pulling it out of his pocket.

As he pulled it from his pocket, a cylinder spiraled upward from the floor. The scientist seemed as surprised as Damien. It contained a slot at its center, which appeared to be for the second key.

"There! Place the key in there! We have to shut this portal down now!" the scientist demanded.

Damien inserted the case of discs into the slot at the cylinder's center without hesitation. Energy flowed from the discs, and then a hologram of a message rose and expanded in the air. Letters shot out in a large halo around the cylinder, and Damien read the message aloud.

"Portal deactivation initiated. Collapse imminent. Bridge to Haven: Deleted."

The projection flowing from the case dimmed and flickered out. Suddenly, glowing green lines appeared on the cylinder, and it abruptly collapsed into the floor. Damien turned toward the portal. The hum dissipated, and the energy no longer touched his face. The portal vanished, and the war of Haven was over.

CHAPTER 14

Planning for the Future

After the portal dissipated, the entire dome became silent. Everyone watched quietly, hoping for it all to be true. After no sign of the portal returning, everyone began cheering. The ones who were well enough rushed to thank Damien. His team were the ones that made it happen.

"I appreciate it," he said. "But it was more than just me. It was my team and everyone on that planet."

They were too celebratory to acknowledge his words, and Damien realized that he had to find his teammates. He noticed Avery giving orders, then being interrupted by a medic with a report. Damien decided not to bother him and went to the nearest doctor on duty.

"Sir, do you know where team SF5-3 is? One of us had a gunshot wound to the chest and was carried through the portal by another group of soldiers."

The doctor glanced at him and thought for a moment. "Go check the emergency room," he said, turning back to the wounded. "They probably took him there. I'm sorry about the other man who was brought in with him. The medics couldn't do anything but take him to the morgue."

Damien knew he was referring to Josiah.

"Thanks," he said. He turned and went to exit the dome. As he approached the door, he turned around to search for Avery, but he was already gone. Damien figured he had business to attend to and might not have been aware of his son's death. As he exited, he realized that he didn't know where the emergency room was. He decided to go to the main lobby to ask. When he entered the lobby, he saw that it was full of news reporters, all probably wanting to know about the latest events. Damien wanted to avoid them. He came up with a plan as he passed a utility closet. He entered it and saw a janitor's suit and cleaning cart. He removed his military attire and put on the suit. He looked like a normal employee.

With the cleaning cart in front of him, Damien walked out of the closet and through the lobby. News reporters glanced at him but immediately turned away. He made his way to a blonde woman at the front desk, who was busy keeping the reporters from moving beyond a certain point.

"Where is the emergency room?"

"This is a launch facility, sir, not a hospital. Once you leave here, there's one right around the corner. Can't miss it."

She returned to managing the reporters, and Damien pushed through the lobby and into the parking lot outside. It was a beautiful sunny day, with many people walking the streets. They were oblivious to the danger they could have been in had his team not succeeded. He searched for the hospital, and it didn't take him long to notice a large white building to his left. People were gathered at its base, and he couldn't tell if they were reporters or not. He would soon find out. He dispatched with the cleaning cart and jogged to the hospital. When he reached the base, he realized that getting through was not going to be an easy task. He attempted to push through anyway.

The crowd of people was simply spectators trying to see some action, trying to get a glimpse of the people who had come back from the other world. Damien pushed through to the front, where there were a doctor and two guards who stood by the entrance of the hospital. Peering through the glass doors, Damien saw that the hospital was packed, and the wounded were waiting in the hallway. When he attempted to go inside, he was stopped by the two guards. The doctor noticed him and addressed him.

"Sorry, sir. You are not allowed past this point. Entrance is for patients and military personnel only."

Damien noticed the doctor staring at his janitor's suit.

"My name is Damien, and I am the leader of SF5-3, the group that delivered the key to shut down the portal. A member of my team was injured and transported here to be treated."

"You look like a janitor to me. I have a hard time believing you," the doctor replied.

Damien didn't want to waste his time trying to prove his identity, and he thought of getting through by force. However, a head popped behind the glass door. It was JD. He called for Damien to come inside, and the doctor realized he was speaking the truth.

"Sorry for the inconvenience, sir."

"It's all right," Damien replied. "You were just doing your job."

He walked passed the doctor and guards and entered the hospital.

"This way," JD said, motioning for him to follow him.

JD weaved through the crowd of patients and made his way to the elevator doors on the opposite end of the hall. Wounded soldiers noticed them and gave weary nods and salutes. Damien also caught many smiles. They were exhausted. They were also glad it was all over. Damien eventually caught up with JD at the elevator.

"He's on the fifth floor."

"How is he?"

"I don't know. The doctor won't tell me anything yet. Once we get there, we'll wait for the news."

Damien was worried by what JD had said. "He better be fine," he said to himself. Peter was the one who brightened the team up. He always found a way to give them a laugh, even in the most serious of situations. They entered the elevator and went to the fifth floor. He proceeded to follow JD. He was glad they were able to get medical attention promptly. It wasn't long before that Peter had been brought through the portal by fellow soldiers. There weren't as many people on the fifth floor, so they didn't have difficulty getting to one of the emergency rooms that resided there. They eventually made it, and there was a row of chairs next to the emergency room door. They both sat down and waited.

Each minute went by slowly and quietly. No sound could be heard beyond the door in front of them. After a long period of waiting, a surgeon emerged from the emergency room. His face looked as if he was going to give them bad news. Damien was shocked and didn't bother listening to the surgeon. He rushed inside the room. On the bed was Peter, sitting comfortably and smiling.

"Gotcha!" Peter said, cheerfully. "You're so gullible."

"Peter . . . that's not funny!" Damien exclaimed. He walked toward Peter as if he was going to smack him across the head, and Peter lifted his arms to protect himself.

"Hey! The doctor said to take it easy," he said with a grin on his face.

"Should you be sitting up?" Damien asked. "You were shot in the chest recently."

"I guess it wasn't too serious."

"What do we do now?" JD asked.

"I'm not sure," Damien replied. "The war on Haven is over, and I'm certain there will be a memorial service for our fallen comrades. We are probably going to be honored in some way also." As he said this, the thought of Moriah came to mind. "I have to get to Moriah and bring her back," he declared.

Just then, Avery came into the room.

"Good, you're all here. I have a few announcements to make, and then I'll leave. First, the memorial will be held three days from now. You will be honored the day after for playing major roles in ending the war. You are off duty until further notice. Go home and be with your families."

"Sir, can I talk to you?" Damien asked before Avery could turn to leave.

"Make it quick; I have a lot of things to attend to, including finding where Josiah went. He might have gone home already, but I figured he would have come to show me he was safe first."

Damien didn't say another word until he and Avery were out in the hallway alone.

"Sir, Josiah didn't make it," he said as he uneasily adjusted his stance and stared at the floor.

"What are you talking about?" The light drained from the man's face as reality was getting ready to pierce his heart.

"The Alpha killed him, and there was nothing I could do. I'm sorry." His words were followed by a long silence.

"So my wife and both of my children," he began, voice low and wavering but filling with rage, "all gone because of that monstrosity. I will find a way to kill that thing no matter the cost. He will pay, and I'll kill him myself."

He left the hallway before Damien could say another word. Damien knew that the man was hurting more than he could imagine. After taking a moment to reflect on events, he went back to his friends. They spent the next hour with Peter.

"Well, Peter, we're going to go ahead and go home," JD said. "We'll visit you often. Make a full recovery."

He left the room, leaving only Damien with Peter. Peter had a sad face and turned to Damien.

"Why did Josiah shoot me?"

"He wasn't himself, Pete," Damien replied. "He was being manipulated. Josiah would never intentionally hurt you."

"Yeah, I know he wouldn't. Where is he? He didn't come to visit me yet. I think he at least owes me that."

Peter had a smirk on his face when he said that, but it disappeared when he saw the look on Damien's face.

"Josiah died, Pete. A Prisoner was controlling him and killed him when he was done using him."

"Oh." Peter's face fell as he turned his head from Damien and stared at the wall.

"I'm sorry, buddy. Are you going to be all right?"

"Yeah," he said softly.

"Well, I'm going to go for now. I'll be back soon."

He patted Peter's shoulder as he said the words. With no reply from Peter, he slowly turned and left the room. He didn't know where to go from that point. Moriah was on a different planet, and the war had left scars that could not be seen on the surface without looking into the eyes of the broken. The war of Haven may have been finished, but the war inside had only begun.

EPILOGUE

The Message

The next few days following the end of the war on Haven felt abnormal. Damien returned to his apartment and waited for the memorial service. That day came and went. Josiah and Moriah were mentioned among the fallen, and his team was honored. Each day was long and uneventful, and Moriah was all he could think about. Avery came to his apartment a week after the memorial service and knocked on the door.

"Damien, are you in there? I have something important to give you."

Damien opened the door and saw that Avery stood there in full military attire. His uniform was improper, almost disheveled. His face looked worn, and his normally clean-shaven face was covered in stubble. He was also holding a touchpad in one hand.

"Avery? What is it? You don't look so well."

"We received a message that can only be opened with a special code," Avery said stiffly, ignoring Damien's concern.

"What makes you think I know it?" he asked, taking the touchpad in hand.

"The message listed you as the receiver. Now that you have it, I'll take my leave. There are still things to clean up."

Damien thought about everything that had happened, but as he began to ask him about his well-being, Avery left, leaving him with the touchpad. He stared at it and wondered who it could be from. He briefly entertained the notion that it was from Moriah, but it could not be. She was in suspended animation in the center of Saturn. As he continued to stare at it, he noticed the entry points for the code. It had enough room to enter a date of some kind. He decided to enter the date that he and Moriah had shared long before, the date they had promised to be together forever. He paused for a brief moment, then pressed the button. Suddenly, a video of Moriah's face appeared on screen. Tears were streaming down her face.

"Damien, I don't know where I am. I can't get out. If you receive this, please save me!"

THE JOURNAL - THE PAST THROUGH ANCIENT EYES

If you are reading this, I am dead. However, I have succeeded in completing my mission. I hope you are reading this under peaceful circumstances. If you are not, I am truly sorry. It is our fault, and as a way of recompense, I will explain how it came to be this way. It began about ten thousand years ago. Life on our world was in danger of extinction. The source of life, our star, was soon going to emit a powerful solar flare. That solar flare was going to head straight for us. We predicted it about one hundred years in advance, and during that time, we searched for ways to avoid destruction. We had previously created another world within a different dimension, its initial purpose being to create and mine resources. We did not foresee it becoming our new home. We had also built a site within Tarnus and had to evacuate from there as well. Nothing within our star system was safe.

We had evacuated our former world and begun a new existence on our new world. It had come to be known as Haven. It saved us from certain death. Since our technology had been biologically based, we knew there would be nothing for us to return to. The only thing that would survive would be the portal, as it was underground and not based on living organisms.

As is the case with human nature, violent disputes unfortunately began. The people of Haven became divided over whether or not it was wise to reopen the portal and return to our former home. A war soon followed. The war was fought between two main groups, the Novus Ordo and the Veteris Ordo. The Novus Ordo were from the south, and the Veteris Ordo were from the north. The Novus Ordo wished to reopen the portal used to enter Haven and return home. However, the Veteris Ordo maintained that reopening the portal would bring about our destruction. The radiation from the solar flare may enter Haven once the portal is opened. After one thousand years, the Novus Ordo began losing the war. Many of their armies died. However, they came up with a solution. They would create a race that would assist them.

The creation of this new race was successful, and they obeyed the Novus Ordo for a time. Soon the race began breeding independently and attacking both the Veteris Ordo and Novus Ordo, and eventually, they were a significant threat. The Novus Ordo and Veteris Ordo decided to join together and contain them. They built prisons, called Nightmare Prisons. Even though their efforts seemed effective at first, they soon realized that the creatures were very crafty and capable of reproducing at an astonishing rate. In order to escape their onslaught, leaders of Haven decided to return to their former world. There was no guarantee that it would be a harmless endeavor. After the preparations were completed, a massive attack led by the unrelenting creatures destroyed most of the population. The remaining survivors fled to the last secure city. Due to limited resources, the survivors within the city did not all have places to sleep. Many slept on the streets, and food eventually became scarce. My personal story began soon after.

I awoke in my dimly lit room and remembered that I was supposed to meet with the leaders. We were going to discuss the final escape plan, one which I hoped would succeed. I walked out to my balcony and observed the city. Many were still sleeping in the streets and on rooftops. There were many hungry. I wanted to end their suffering, and if the plan worked, my desire would be realized within a few days. I left my room and went down the building's gravity suspension elevator. It took me to the lobby, where some high-ranking individuals were present. I met one of the leaders, Paul, who was to take me to the final meeting. His countenance seemed sad upon approaching him.

"What's wrong?" I asked.

"Nothing. Are you ready to leave?"

"Yes."

I followed him out of the building and noticed the control center that towered over us, my final destination. We did not exchange words while we walked to the tower, and as I avoided stepping on the countless people lying in the streets, I heard gunshots and beastly screams from outside the city. I could never grow used to the situation. We made it to the base of the tower, and it was heavily guarded as usual. There were active turrets on its walls designed to eradicate any of those ferocious creatures. We entered the elevator to go to the uppermost room. The man who was leading the way seemed to be acting strangely. He didn't speak a word the entire time, but perhaps it was due to the dire circumstances. We reached the top of the tower and followed the stairs to the hallway that led to the control room. After we were scanned, we entered the room.

All seven leaders were present, with Kent, the man who led them, standing near the windows. He was looking out at the city.

He turned from the windows as he noticed my arrival. "Good," Kent announced. "Everyone is here. Let's get started." He motioned for me to take a seat.

Paul and I sat in the two remaining seats.

One of the leaders spoke. "We are ready to initiate the mass evacuation to the portal on the other side of the planet. If everything goes according to plan, we should have minimum casualties."

"What is our plan again?" Kent asked, looking at everyone.

Another leader stood. "Sir, we plan to use our underground transport system to travel to the portal. Our investigations found that most systems have been damaged or occupied by the enemy, but there are enough to evacuate the city in a single day."

"It sounds simple enough," Kent replied. He looked at a hologram displayed over the center of the table. It showed the underground transport systems currently accessible. "What if we encounter the enemy?"

"We are building defensive turrets on the transports as we speak," said one leader seated right next to me. "The turrets will be strong enough to handle any obstacle. We just need firepower above ground."

As the discussion carried on, I began to wonder what would happen. I did not believe that we were going to close off this dimension forever. We would probably wait until every last one of the creatures died before returning. Perhaps we wouldn't come back until we had the means to handle them more efficiently.

Kent continued, "Once we return to our former world, we will rebuild from the bottom up. Our cities have doubtlessly vanished from the passing of time and the initial blast from the sun. We will return to the way of living our ancestors used to follow when they first began. We will certainly survive. Future generations will have a way to return to Haven. The portal shall remain active, and the key needed to shut it down will be passed down. The portal, manufactured by our ancestors, has but one flaw. Without the key, the portal will remain open for five years before shutting down. We in this room are the only ones who have the code to unlock the key." He turned to face the windows once again. "We will begin evacuation tomorrow. We, the leaders, will be the last ones to leave. We are in charge of making sure the plan is carried out. However, one of us will come back to shut down the portal. The portal shall remain inoperative until the other side is shut down. Once that is done, the portal will be activated once more, allowing access from our home world. Regrettably, the one who performs this deeply important task will not be able to return with us. They will have a single pod, one located in this room, that will take them to Tarnus where they will wait in sleep until we reclaim all that we left behind."

The entire room was silent. I suspected that everyone wondered who would carry out such a task. I thought about the suffering happening within the city. Many were hungry and unsheltered. As I thought about this, I had a sudden urge, an urge to rescue everyone from their suffering. I volunteered to carry out the task.

"I'll do it," I said aloud.

There was no immediate reaction. Everyone remained quiet. Paul then broke the silence.

"I'll escort him," he said. "He'll need help making it back, and if two of us go, we have a better chance of succeeding. I'll sacrifice myself for the sake of humanity." He looked over to me.

"It is decided then," Kent announced. "This meeting is adjourned. Get a good night's sleep. The upcoming days won't be easy."

I thought about what I had just volunteered to do, and I wondered if I wanted Paul to join me in such a mission. Kent told everyone to clean the room one last time and left. We put away the chairs except the master chair in front of the hologram. I suppose we cleaned it for future generations to see. After that was done, I left the room. I decided to take the stairs instead of the elevator. I wanted to clear my head. When I exited the tower, I smiled at the sight of the people in the city. Their suffering would soon end. I went along the streets and told many people that they would soon be able to return to our former home. I wanted to give them hope. Many were greatly encouraged, and some even ran down the streets with joy, spreading the good news.

I returned to my room, and there was still plenty of time left before the day's end, but there was nothing important for me to do. I did not have a family anymore. So I decided to take Kent's advice and lay down to sleep early. I did not dream that night, and I awoke at dawn. I walked to my bedroom window and looked over the city again. Early risers could be seen dancing in the streets. I smiled at the sight and got ready to go back to the tower. I was greeted with smiles on my way there. Some were waiting for me at the base of the tower, ready to begin the evacuation. The leaders were gathered around a podium at the steps of the building. The people of the city slowly gathered around the area. There was a lot of chatter, but when I took my place among the leaders, the crowd grew silent. The cries of the enemy from outside the city were the only thing heard. Kent stood behind the podium, ready to give a speech that would be heard throughout the city.

"People of Haven, today is the day of our journey to a lost freedom. Today is the day we return to our former world." Cheering erupted from the crowd. "But first, we need to make that journey."

The ground began to vibrate, and the stairs separated and revealed steps leading underground. Brilliant green light flowed from it.

Kent continued, "In an orderly fashion, please begin your way down. Once you have reached the bottom, you will be guided on what you will need to do. Our evacuation is expected to take three days at most. Please be patient."

I watched everyone slowly make their way down the steps. Kent turned to me.

"I want you to be on the first transport out of here. Be on the other end to make sure everyone gets through safely. When the last group is coming,

I'll send a message telling you to come back and complete your mission. Do you understand?"

He gazed into my eyes as if he expected me to falter. "Yes, I understand," I told him.

It was a good plan, and I was prepared to do my part. I did not worry about my inevitable circumstance. I concerned myself with helping everyone return home. The leaders were to take a different stairway underground, and I soon made it to the underground chamber that contained the transports, which were hovering over the pathways. Each side of a transport had three entry points. None of the civilians were there yet. Military troops poured into the dome and occupied the transports. Their mission was to secure the path of evacuation. Each was heavily armed with our best available weapons. The transport disappeared down the tunnel, and other transports appeared, fitted with guns on both the front and back. Once civilians reached the area, they were escorted into the transports. Once they were full, the transports lifted and moved down the tunnel. I noticed that some of the passengers were carrying certain items. Some had tents, and others had food. Everyone tried to bring as much as they could with them to survive. They did not know what the other world was like, and neither did I. An old man sat next to me. He appeared as someone who needed a much-deserved rest. He was busily rummaging through a bag in his lap, and I noticed some things in his bag that many would regard as quite primitive. He had a set of flint rocks, a magnifying glass, and a long string wound up with metal hooks.

"I hope it's safe on the other side," he said.

I turned to him. "I'm sure it will be," I said.

"How do you know?" he asked, searching my face for an answer.

"It's faith," I replied. That was the only reply I could give. He seemed content with it.

"Then I shall have faith in your faith," he said, showing a slight grin. He went back to searching his bag.

I encouraged him, and that was what I wanted to do. I spent most of the ride trying to comfort others. Some were easier to comfort than others. In fact, some were not able to be comforted, but others were glad to see someone have a caring attitude. Eventually, an announcement came through the transport's intercom system.

"Our journey is one-third of the way complete," the announcement began. "We will be stopping the transports to charge. From there, we will proceed to the next destination within five hours. Please get plenty of rest in the meantime."

The announcement ended. I looked out one of windows, and there was nothing but darkness staring back at me. The thought of a deadly beast lurking within it crept up. The thought terrified me. To get rid of the feeling, I went and lay down for a nap. My dream was of a world of paradise, a world without pain and suffering. The utopia had my long-lost family, and everyone was at ease. There were smiles on every face. A bloodcurdling scream awoke me. I felt the transport lunge forward, and I immediately looked out the window. To my horror, one of those dangerous creatures was running alongside us. Passengers screamed and moved away from one side of the transport. Suddenly, it burst into particles as it was shot by the dematerialization cannon fitted to the transport. The transport was soon moving just as it was before. Everyone slowly calmed down, but it was obvious they were all afraid and nervous. I had to do something to comfort them. I stood.

"Listen, I know that you're scared, but there is nothing to be afraid of. We are safe. No one was harmed, and it will remain that way. We have planned for these situations. This will soon be all behind you. Look forward to that. Be brave, and together we will make it through." I sat back down, and everyone continued to look at me. I said one more thing. "Pass it on."

At first, it didn't seem that I was successful in making a difference, but the old man from earlier stood.

"I will pass on those words to as many people as I can. I thank you for giving them to me. I am sure many will find hope in them." He smiled at me and moved to the next compartment.

The journey was very long, but we finally reached our destination. We were not attacked a second time. The passengers seemed to become excited as we got closer to the final point. As we reached the final stop, troops greeted us and began escorting us to the portal. With me in front, they led us to the surface. We exited a small facility that seemed to be within a valley. We moved through the valley and into a forest. I was sure we were in safe hands, but I kept my eyes open for the enemy. Some could have been lurking in the trees while we traversed the forest. We soon came to the city. The large gate was open, and I was fearful.

"Why is the gate already open, and why is everything going so smoothly?" I asked, not expecting immediate answers.

As we walked through the gate, the soldiers turned to the crowd.

"Do not panic," one said. "There are fallen soldiers ahead. It has been confirmed that the area is safe. We ask that you wait while we activate the portal." He spoke into his communicator. "Begin activation of the portal."

Activating the portal had to be done from the control tower, and after a moment, it seemed that everything went smoothly.

"Please proceed!" a soldier commanded. "Be prepared to occupy our ancient home."

The crowd followed behind, but I was pulled aside by one of the soldiers.

"Sir, you have orders to return to the control tower," she said.

Indeed. That was what I had volunteered to do. I would not be able to go with everyone else. I looked on as the crowd moved forward without me.

"All right," I replied.

I looked at the city once more, then turned to begin my journey back to the transport. After looking around, I found that Paul wasn't with me. It was then that I knew Paul had proceeded to the portal. The man was never much of a hero. He wanted to be one but always put himself first. He only liked the notion.

"I will escort you, sir," the soldier said with a smiling face.

Since Paul wasn't around, I welcomed her company but warned her of what joining me would mean for her. Regardless of the approaching death, she agreed without hesitation. She was a soldier; I don't know what else I expected. The journey back to the transports was quiet initially, but she eventually started up a conversation.

"So, why didn't you just go to our installation on Tarnus?"

"We thought about it, but we concluded that we would have a better chance of survival on our world," I replied. "It has oxygen and plenty of resources. Tarnus does not have the same conditions, although there are various structures built by us there. It would be unsustainable. I'm sure we will return one day. Our safety pods are set to launch there."

She put on a confused look. "Safety pods set to launch on Tarnus?"

"Yes, but they have become impractical. They are scattered all over, and we would lose more people if we were to attempt to retrieve them. We were going to use them quite some time ago, but our efforts were unfruitful. They remain unused to this day."

She didn't seem to have any other questions. We reached the facility, which led underground. Crowds of people continually left from there. We waited for transport to take us back, and onlookers gave us confused stares. After watching a large number of civilians leave the transport, a transport that would take me back became available.

"I guess this is it," I said, standing up and walking to the transport.

"So you're the one who is going to perform the most important duty?"

"Yes, you can say that."

I walked to the transport and entered it along with my companion. I asked her one last time if this was what she truly wanted.

Her green, compassionate eyes looked into mine. "I can't let you do it alone," she said.

Her selfless act astonished me. "Thank you," I said to her.

As I sat with her in the transport, I thought about why she decided to come with me instead of moving on with everyone else. Surely she knew what lay ahead. I never determined her reason, and perhaps that was for the best. On our way back, I heard an explosion, but it didn't seem to affect us. Then not long after, as we were getting close to the city, our transport crashed into something. It was something large enough to stop us, but it did not cause major damage on the inside. I stood and looked out the window. It was dark; then the transport lights lit the surrounding area. I found that we were at a loading station just outside the city. My heart was pounding in my chest as I looked around. I turned to the soldier, and her face revealed that she had the same thing in mind. Something was forcing us to leave the transport. We waited in the transport, hoping that it would start moving again. It never did. We hesitantly left the transport and had to make the rest of the journey back on foot.

"I think we should take the tunnel the rest of the way," I said.

"That's not a good idea," she said. "It's too enclosed. If there is an ambush or something, we wouldn't have a chance."

She had a point. It would take longer, but the surface route would be safer. We had to determine what had stopped us and if it was dangerous.

Moreover, we had to determine whether it was still around or not. We communicated in whispers.

"If it's an enemy, it would probably be a C5," I said.

"That makes sense," she replied. "It would certainly need to be quite large and strong enough to stop the transport, and it's underground. It may be a nest builder, and if so, we are in great danger. Wherever there is a nest, there are many of them."

The thought was deeply disturbing. The only creature that was capable of making elaborate plans and such was the C-ZERO. This was the highest class within the ranking system we devised for the creatures.

"Nest builders are typically nonaggressive. We shouldn't have much trouble with it," I said.

"You're right," she replied. "We should be able to make our way to the top, if it's just a nest builder. If it's not, have this just in case." She pulled out a pistol and handed it to me.

I slowly took the weapon. "Thanks," I said.

I'd never used a weapon before, and I wasn't sure I was ready to use one. She crouched down and moved to the exit. After scanning the area, she hit the emergency button. As the door opened, she went out and swept the area with her weapon, one which seemed to be some type of automatic weapon. She turned and signaled to come join her. The stairs that led to the surface were not far. We made our way to the stairs and, due to the limited lighting provided by the transport, we found that they led to complete darkness. Fear entered my heart. I did not know what to expect.

"It'll be fine," she said. "I have night vision lenses. Just stay close to me, and we'll make it in no time."

"What if we're attacked?"

"I'd hold it off while you flee to safety," she replied without hesitation.

She put on her lenses and started up the stairs. I stayed very close to her and held onto a backpack she was wearing. I felt very vulnerable due to the darkness, but as long as I stayed close, I had some reassurance. She was willing to risk her life to save me, and I was not sure I would do the same, at the time. We eventually reached the top, and I became calm. The daylight was both beautiful and comforting.

"There," she said, removing her lenses. "That wasn't so bad now, was it?" I grew fond of her smile.

"I'd rather not do it again," I said.

The area was surrounded by very tall trees, a place where screaming C1 enemies could be lurking. They tended to work in packs. A scream was heard in the distance, which worried me a bit.

"We should get moving," she said.

I didn't argue with the suggestion. We started walking in the direction of the city, slowly making our way through the forest, trying not to bring attention to ourselves. We soon came to the field before the city's front bridge. We did not encounter any enemies, and that fact made us wary. The soldier surveyed the expanse of open field then turned to me.

"We're going to run to the city."

"Okay," I said, gazing into her green eyes.

We ran toward the bridge, and as we approached it, something unexpected appeared. Coming out from behind the bridge was a figure in a dark hood. It was the C-ZERO. We came to a halt. His red eyes were fixed on us.

"Come closer, Donovan," he said.

I obeyed him out of fear. As I began to walk to him, I was stopped. My hand was clenched and pulled.

"Don't do it," the soldier said.

A grin came across the C-ZERO's face. "I'm only here to talk," he said. "Can't you at least hear me out?"

"What do you want?" I said.

"To tell you why," he replied.

"Tell me why? Why what?" I replied. I struggled to keep my composure.

"Why I haven't killed you and why I have allowed all of you to leave. Why we did not attack to kill, and why I made you come to the surface," he announced.

"I don't understand. Explain."

"Oh, quite demanding, aren't we? It is quite simple. The long war has greatly diminished our population, as it has yours. Continuing the war would lead to mutual extinction. We decided to stop attacking and to rebuild instead. I am aware of your duty, Donovan. It is to shut down the portal and save your people. However, your kind is a curious bunch, and you will eventually return. We will be ready then, but they will not know of it until our final attack. Things are forgotten as time progresses, and this surely will be, too. Your kind are mortal, and I am not. I will be here waiting for your kind to return. Leave and save your kind, but your safety is not forever."

He stepped aside to let us pass. We were speechless and did not move for a moment, but we regained our senses and ran to the bridge. As we moved toward the city, the soldier's grip on my hand was lost. A pop was heard. I turned to her, and she was on the ground, clutching her side. I turned to the C-ZERO and saw that he had a gun in hand. He smiled and disappeared. I was angry, but I had to focus on my companion. Her side was soaked in blood. I had to do something.

"Just hang on," I said.

I picked her up and started to carry her across the bridge. She gripped tightly to my arms, but it soon faded as we came closer to the city gate. We entered the gate, and we made our way to the tower. The streets were clear. Her breathing became slower, and all I could do was encourage her to hang in there. I made it to the control tower and took the elevator to the control room. As I watched my companion steadily fade in my arms, a tear ran down my cheek. Her blood began soaking into my shirt. She was close to death. She opened her eyes and tried to speak to me, but nothing came from her mouth.

"Save your strength," I whispered.

She nodded and closed her eyes again. We reached the top of the tower and went to the control room. I had to act fast once I was inside the control room. I rushed to a transport tube within the room and opened it. A personal escape pod was inside. I laid her in the seat within the pod and securely strapped her in. I shut the chamber. The door became transparent, allowing me to see her. She barely opened her eyes, showing me that she was still alive.

"Computer," I said, "put subject in suspended animation and transport her to a safe location on Tarnus. Resume animation when more than one person is present to watch over her. Until someone is there, I want her wounds to heal."

She looked at me as I gave those commands.

"Anything else, sir?" the computer responded.

"Yes," I said. "Lock down this section of the city. Allow only humans to enter. Keep up defenses and keep this tower secure. That is all."

A tear came down the soldier's cheek. She lifted a hand and began writing on the door. As her fingers moved across the surface, green light shown through the glass and lit up her final words.

"My name's Sarah. Thank you for saving me and humanity. I'll never forget you."

I smiled and nodded, showing that I understood. She lowered her hand, and the suspended animation process began. She slowly closed her eyes, with a smile on her face. The pod was launched, and I went to the window and searched the sky. Her pod, wrapped in light, climbed into the sky and soon vanished. She was safe. I had one final thing to accomplish, and I sat down in the head chair.

"Computer, bring the camera up to the portal." A holographic video appeared over the table displaying the portal.

All of the civilians had successfully evacuated, and all that remained were the soldiers who guarded the portal. They were waiting for me. "Give them the green light, computer." When the soldiers received the notification, they went through the portal. I was then the only man in the world. I initiated the shutdown of the portal, and it soon vanished. There were two lights on the table in front of me, one red and one green. The green light indicated that the portal on our world's side was still active. It became red after a few moments. When it did, I turned the display to the portal once more. This left only one green light, and that was mine. I accomplished my mission. As I finish my account of the final events of my life, I cannot help but wonder what will become of this world. I continue to think about what the C-ZERO said. I am not worried, however. We are a strong-willed race, and we will certainly win. For the future humanity that finds this place, I have placed the key in the locked compartment. The access code is . . .